SUNRISE ISLAND CELEBRATIONS

SUNRISE ISLAND SERIES
BOOK 4

MAREN HILL

1

KYLA

July, 2023

Kyla sat very still, afraid even the shift of her breath might wake the baby, and watched Isabella's tiny chest rise and fall. Each soft inhale, each quiet exhale, steadied something deep inside her in a way she hadn't expected.

How could I be so lucky?

Afternoon sunlight streamed through the west window toward Clay's paragliding school. Moving carefully, she reached for the organic cotton sleeper she'd set aside after Isabella's bath and eased one tiny foot inside. Izzy stirred, sighing softly, but didn't wake as Kyla gently guided the sleeper over her diaper and gently worked it up over her shoulders and arms.

Even though she craved sleep, Kyla sometimes had to resist the urge to wake her—just to see those wide eyes, to hear the soft coos that already felt like conversation. Watching her sleep brought a quiet kind of peace, but it was those waking moments she treasured most.

As she gazed down at Izzy, that familiar jolt returned. There was no denying who her daughter resembled.

Nearly seven months had passed since Kyla and Jude had parted—nothing like the bittersweet farewell she'd once imagined. She pushed the thought aside, refusing to let it intrude on this fragile, perfect calm. What stayed with her instead was the moment the nurse had placed her newborn against her chest, that tiny weight anchoring her to a new reality. And even then, in that first breathless instant, she had seen it—the unmistakable resemblance.

A rhythmic knock at the cottage door drew her back.

Harry had been patient, honoring her wish to let the Mitchell family savor these first few days alone. It had been twenty-five years since a newborn had joined the family, and everyone wanted to soak it in. Now, with Izzy still asleep and the cottage quiet, Kyla felt ready to share this new part of her life with him.

"Shhh," she said, opening the door, one finger pressed to her lips.

Harry smiled, lowering his voice. "Not the warmest welcome, sweetheart—but I'm guessing the little one's asleep."

"She is," Kyla said, unable to hide her smile. "And I can't wait for you to meet her."

He stepped inside, his expression softening as he took her in. "You look amazing, Kye." He handed her a neatly wrapped package tied with a silk ribbon.

"Aw, thank you." She glanced down at herself with a small laugh. "I'll feel more like me soon." Then, lifting the gift slightly, she added," Did you wrap this?"

Harry chuckled. "No, I had help. Your sister took charge—picked it out, and made sure it looked like that.

Glancing toward the bassinet, he moved closer on quiet feet. His smile widened as he looked down at Izzy, her tiny fists tucked beneath the sleeves of her sleeper.

"She's beautiful," he whispered. "I can't wait to hold her.

Kyla stepped beside him. "Ever held a newborn before?"

"Newborn puppies, kittens... rabbits ...he said under his breath. "But, no—first time with a human."

Kyla smiled. "Same here. I'm learning as I go."

After a few more moments, they moved to the settee. Harry leaned in closer, brushing a soft kiss against her lips. "I hope you'll let me be part of this," he said quietly.

"Of course," Kyla said, though her tone softened. "Just... slowly. It's all so new. For both of us."

Harry nodded, his gaze dropping for a moment before returning to hers. "I know. And I'm not in a hurry." He reached for her hand. "I just want to be there for her—for both of you. However, you need me. "

His words settled between them, gentle but weighted. He knew everything—how Jude had reacted when she'd told him about the pregnancy. The rejection. The accusations. The question that had cut deeper than anything else.

Are you planning on keeping the baby?

That chapter was closed. Their only connection now was the occasional message—like the one that had arrived just days after Izzy's birth.

Hey, Sundance! Are you a mama yet? I think your due date's around now. Let me know—boy or girl? —Jude

She had read it twice, then set her phone aside.

He'd kept his distance, just as they'd agreed.

That was enough.

Kyla unwrapped the gift and lifted a delicate dress with a layered skirt. "This is beautiful, Harry. I love it."

"Our little princess," he said softly.

Kyla didn't answer, only smiled as she folded the dress across her lap.

"I figured flowers would be unnecessary," he added. "Your gardens will be doing the job soon enough."

She laughed. "True. And how lucky am I—to have a

summer baby?" Her gaze drifted back to the bassinet. "I couldn't be happier. I'm really glad you're here."

"Listen," Harry whispered suddenly. "She's waking up." He moved toward the bassinet, but Kyla reached her first, lifting Izzy gently into her arms.

"They feel like jelly at first," she said with a soft laugh. "And always support the baby's head—neck muscles aren't strong enough yet.

Harry smiled. "And the soft spot?"

"Okay, you know a little, she teased. "Yes—gentle."

He sat, and Kyla carefully placed Izzy in his arms. She watched his face soften, something almost reverent in the way he held her.

"There's a picture," Kyla murmured.

Then Izzy let out a sharp cry.

Harry's expression shifted instantly. "She sounds so... fragile. And loud.

Kyla laughed softly. "You've done nothing wrong." She checked the diaper, then shook her head. "She's hungry."

"She sounds so fragile... and loud," Harry said, eyes wide.

She adjusted her top and brought Izzy to her breast. The baby latched, and Kyla winced slightly before settling.

"Is it uncomfortable?" Harry asked.

"Only when I overdo it," she said lightly. "I'm still figuring it out."

Harry watched them both, as if the moment might vanish if he looked away.

Kyla felt it too—that fragile, impossible sense that everything had changed... and nothing was certain.

Two Weeks Later

Rollo's bark shattered the quiet as a stranger pedaled up the long gravel driveway of the Mitchell farm. Clay glanced up from the barn, squinting at the figure dismounting near the turnaround. Rollo's tail wagged hesitantly as the man crouched to rub his ears.

"Hey there, boy," the man said, his hand lingering on Rollo's scruff.

Clay crossed the barnyard, Music's bridle swinging by his side. "Can I help you?"

The man rose to his full height and offered his hand. "I'm Jude—the baby's father," he said, flashing a grin that lingered a bit too long.

Clay's grip tightened on the bridle, leather creaking in his hand. His gaze shifted toward Kyla's cottage. "Is Kyla expecting you?"

"Nope. Thought I'd surprise her." Jude's grin held—too easy, too comfortable.

Clay's brow creased. "She's in for a surprise, that's for sure. Wait here. I'll check if she's up for visitors."

Jude sprawled on the grass, and Rollo flopped down beside him. Clay knocked lightly on Kyla's door. She opened it wrapped in a towel, her hair damp.

"Jude's outside," Clay said. "Wants to see you. And the baby." His voice softened. "Want me to send him away?"

Kyla's hand tightened around the doorframe. "I didn't know he was coming." Anger flared—quick and hot—, but she forced it down. "No, it's fine. I'll see him. Give me fifteen minutes."

Clay delivered the message, adding, "Why don't you take a walk to the corral? I think our palomino mare could use some company." Jude nodded and strode off with Rollo in tow.

Kyla took her time getting dressed. It felt like another life—the day she'd planned to tell him. She'd imagined it happening here, in this cottage, where they would build something together. Instead, it had unraveled into something she still couldn't fully name.

She tucked Izzy into her carrier and headed outside. She'd keep the visit brief—and leave the moment she felt the need.

The sight of Jude leaning against the fence pulled at something she'd tried to bury. Sun-darkened skin, wind-tossed hair, that crooked, too-familiar smile—

She approached cautiously. Jude turned, his smile widening. "Hey there, Sundance. Gorgeous as ever."

Kyla stopped short. "It's Kyla. Not Sundance. That life's over."

Jude laughed, raising his hands in mock surrender. "Got it. Kyla, it is." His eyes drifted to Izzy. He shifted forward as if resisting the urge to reach out. "I've waited a long time to see her," he said, his eyes softening.

"Let's walk to the orchard," Kyla said. "And next time, give me a heads-up. I want you in Izzy's life, but I need notice."

Jude nodded. "Fair enough. I thought that surprising you might be fun. Turns out, not my best idea."

As they walked among the cherry and peach trees, a sense of calmness replaced the tension of moments ago. When they reached the wooden bench, Kyla slid the right carrier strap off her shoulder.

"Here, let me help," Jude offered as he lifted the carrier and set it on the bench.

Kyla lifted Izzy and moved her close to Jude.

Jude spoke softly. "Is this...our Izzy?" He took her gently, his hands trembling slightly. "Come to Daddy, little princess."

Watching Izzy's father meet her for the first time in the family orchard filled Kyla with warmth, but confusion lingered. This wasn't the man who had told her to *take care of it.*

Or maybe it was—and that was worse.

Kyla crossed her arms, uncertain how to reconcile the tenderness in his voice with the memory of his rejection.

Jude cradled Izzy carefully, his thumb brushing over her tiny fingers. "She's beautiful," he whispered.

Kyla gave a small nod. "She looks like you. People just don't know it yet."

He smiled at that, and for a moment, neither of them spoke.

The breeze drifted through the orchard, carrying the scent of ripening fruit, and for a moment—just a moment—Kyla let herself imagine a different version of this day.

Then she shut it down.

"How was your visit with Jude?" Jennie asked.

Kathleen perked up, leaning forward in her favorite chair on the verandah. The sunset stretched across the sky in a deep orange-red band, heat lingering in the air even as the day slipped away.

"I have to admit, it was... nice." Kyla smiled, a soft laugh escaping. "Since he showed up unannounced, I didn't have time to overthink it."

Her gaze drifted as she replayed the afternoon. "What surprised me was how excited he was about Izzy. Mom, I hope you don't mind that I didn't bring him to meet you both..."

"Not at all, dear. When the time is right—if it ever feels right—we'll look forward to it," Jennie said gently, though her eyes lingered on Kyla a moment longer than usual.

"Will he be visiting often?" Kathleen asked.

Kyla shrugged. "Hard to say. You know how his work is— one organic farm to the next, wherever the wind takes him. Half the time, he doesn't even know where he'll land."

"Ah," Jennie said with a small nod. "A free spirit."

"That's one way to put it," Kyla replied, a hint of dry amusement in her voice.

"Not exactly father material," Kathleen added.

Kyla let out a quiet laugh. "No... not exactly."

She hesitated, then added, "He did say he'd be working at

EarthSong for the summer. "Wants to spend as much time with Izzy as he can while he's here."

That earned a small shift in Jennie's expression—barely there, but present. "Earthsong," she repeated softly.

Kyla noticed it. "It's only temporary," she said quickly. "Just while he's passing through."

Jennie nodded, but her gaze stayed thoughtful. "Of course."

A brief silence settled, broken only by the distant sound of crickets starting up in the orchard.

Kyla chuckled. "Maybe. But with Jude, I'm keeping my expectations low. I'm just glad he came to meet her. Beyond that, it's anyone's guess."

Kathleen perked up, leaning forward in her favourite chair on the verandah. The sunset stretched across the sky in a deep orange-red band, heat lingering in the air even as the day slipped away.

"I have to admit, it was... nice." Kyla smiled, a soft laugh slipping out. "Since he showed up unannounced, I didn't have time to overthink it." Her gaze drifted as she replayed the afternoon. "What surprised me was how excited he was about Izzy. Mom, I hope you don't mind that I didn't bring him over to meet you both..."

"Not at all, dear. When the time is right—if it ever feels right—we'll look forward to it," Jennie said gently, though her eyes lingered on Kyla a moment longer than usual.

"Will he be visiting often?" Kathleen asked.

Kyla shrugged. "Hard to say. You know how his work is— one organic farm to the next, wherever the wind takes him. Half the time, he doesn't even know where he'll land."

"Ah," Jennie said with a small nod. "A free spirit."

"That's one way to put it," Kyla replied, a hint of dry amusement in her voice.

"Not exactly father material," Kathleen added.

Kyla let out a quiet laugh. "No... not exactly."

She hesitated, then added, "He did say he'll be working at EarthSong for the summer. Wants to spend as much time with Izzy as he can while he's here."

That earned a small shift in Jennie's expression—barely there, but present. "EarthSong," she repeated softly.

Kyla noticed it. "It's only temporary," she said quickly. "Just while he's passing through."

Jennie nodded, but her gaze stayed thoughtful. "Of course."

A brief silence settled, broken only by the distant sound of crickets starting up in the orchard.

Kyla smoothed a hand over her skirt. "I'm just keeping things simple. I'm glad he came to meet her. Beyond that..." She gave a small shrug. "We'll see."

Kathleen hummed softly, settling back into her chair again, but Jennie's attention remained on Kyla for a moment longer—measured, unreadable.

"Just make sure," Jennie said at last, her tone still gentle, "that 'simple' stays simple."

Kyla's smile held, but it tightened at the edges. "It will."

SEEING Harry so soon after Jude's visit only sharpened the contrast between them. With his neatly trimmed beard and dark-rimmed designer glasses, Harry carried himself with an easy polish. At thirty-one, he'd been practicing as a vet for six years.

Jude, at twenty-three, untethered and indifferent to careers, seemed perfectly content drifting from one place to the next.

For Kyla, the difference that mattered now was simple: one wanted a family—and one had made it clear he didn't.

You can't change people, she thought.

And yet... hadn't she seen it happen? Harry had gone from gruff employer to passionate lover in the space of a single day.

A flash of white cut through her thoughts as Harry's shiny F-150 circled the turnaround. They'd planned Izzy's first hike—an easy coastal trail, just an hour there and back.

"We're almost ready, babe," Kyla said, greeting him with a quick kiss. "Do you mind setting up Izzy's car seat while I grab a few more things?"

"Sure thing." Harry lifted the car seat and headed back outside. "Let's swing by the Sunrise Café first. My coffee maker's dead, and I'm feeling it."

They waved to Kathleen as they headed down the driveway.

"Nice to get out of the house," Kyla said. "Perfect day for a hike."

"I'm honoured to be part of such a milestone," Harry said lightly. "First hike—definitely one for the baby book, right, Kye?"

"It is," Kyla said, smiling. "I hope she grows up loving island life... stays here, carries on the family legacy."

"I've never met a Mitchell who didn't," Harry said as he pulled in near the café.

He reached for the door handle—then paused at a knock on Kyla's window.

A young man with wind-tossed hair stood there, motioning for her to roll it down.

Instead, Kyla opened the door. "Hey—Jude..." She winced. "Sorry. You must get that all the time."

"Not nearly enough," Jude said, grinning. His gaze slid past her, searching for the baby through the tinted glass. "Funny—I could've sworn I just saw you yesterday."

Harry rounded the truck, a polite half-smile in place. "Hello, I don't think we've met."

"I'm Jude—Izzy's father. He held out his hand.

Kyla felt it before she saw it—the shift. Harry's expression didn't change, but something tightened beneath it.

"You can imagine," Kyla said quickly, "this is a bit unexpected."

"Not unexpected," Harry said evenly. "Just new information." He shook Jude's hand. "I didn't realize you were on the island. Are you here long?"

"All summer," Jude said easily. "Don't get many chances to see my daughter. Figured I'd make the most of it."

Harry nodded once. "Of course." He turned to Kyla. "Want anything?"

"No, I'm good."

"I'll be right back."

Kyla watched him walk into the cafe—his stride just a fraction more rigid than before.

"So," Jude said, as if nothing had shifted, "what are you three up to today?"

"We're going for a hike," Kyla said. "Izzy's first."

"Nice," Jude smiled. "Plenty more where that came from. We should take her up Mount Maxwell sometime. Or those fairy doors on Mount Erskine—kids love that."

Kyla laughed. "Why don't we start with the West Coast Trail? Never too early, right?"

Jude grinned.

Harry returned just as her laughter faded. He slid into the driver's seat, started the engine, and took a sip of his coffee without speaking.

"Mmm, that smells good," Kyla said lightly.

No response.

He shifted into reverse, giving Jude a brief nod.

"Bye," Kyla said quickly, closing the door as Jude stepped back from the truck. He lifted a hand in a loose wave as they pulled away.

Silence settled between them.

Kyla glanced at Harry. She'd seen flashes of his temper at the clinic—enough to know this quiet wasn't nothing.

"Look," she said carefully, "I'm sorry you had to meet Jude like that. He can be... abrupt. Especially about announcing he's Izzy's father."

Harry let out a short breath. "Yeah. He's got a style."

He took another sip of coffee, eyes fixed on the road.

"The Chris Hatfield Trail's a good choice," he added after a moment. "Easy. Flat. Good for today."

Kyla studied him, then nodded. "Sounds perfect."

TRAMPING ALONG THE SHORT BOARDWALK, they turned left toward Cusheon Cove, where the water shimmered softly in the sunlight. Harry slipped the straps from his shoulders and set the carrier in a cozy spot, his gaze drifting to the waves beyond.

No sooner had they settled than Harry remarked, "If I'd seen Jude in town—without knowing who he was—I think I'd have guessed."

Kyla stilled, her breath catching for a moment. "What do you mean?"

"Izzy looks so much like him," Harry said, his gaze fixed on the horizon.

Kyla hesitated as a touch of unease slipped in. "Does that bother you, honey?"

"Nah. My sister's kids changed so much growing up—almost daily, it seemed." His tone stayed casual, his gaze on the water.

"I see," A small laugh slipped out. "So, you're hoping Izzy takes after me in the end?"

Harry pulled Kyla close, a grin spreading across his face. "The more like you, the better."

They strolled along the gravelly, driftwood-strewn beach, taking in the rocky hills and tangled forest. A sailboat glided across the water, its white sail a quiet symbol of leisure. Reaching the boardwalk, they turned right toward Yeo Point.

"You know," Kyla said, "we should come back next spring when the daffodils bloom. It's quite a sight."

"I've heard," Harry said. "Izzy will be almost a year old by then."

Kyla smiled softly. "Hard to imagine. She let the thought settle, her hand resting lightly on the carrier, her gaze still on the water."Amazing how much can change in a year—how different things can feel."

As Kyla entered the cottage carrying two pieces of Kathleen's homemade raspberry pie, she raised her brows, watching Jude change Izzy's diaper.

"I bounced, cuddled, and walked her around the breezeway, but she still wouldn't settle. I couldn't figure out what was wrong until, well, let's say she didn't pass the sniff test."

Kyla set the dessert dishes on her kitchen table and moved closer to the changing table. "You did that like a pro," she said. "I have to say I'm impressed."

Jude smiled awkwardly, then lifted Izzy and handed her to Kyla. "Look at that," he said, as the baby kicked her feet at the sight of her mother.

"Holding her feels... different from what I thought it would," Jude murmured, his gaze distant for a fleeting second before he smiled again.

Kyla placed Izzy in her baby rocker and positioned it near the kitchen table.

"Just wait until you taste Grandma's raspberry pie. I warmed it up to bring out the flavor even more."

Jude took a bite and let out a low hum. "Mmm. This is unbelievable, Kye. Your grandma's an amazing cook." He scraped the plate clean. "If you weren't here, babe—" He stopped abruptly, exhaled through his nose, and gave a sheepish smirk. "Sorry, Kye. That just slipped out. I didn't mean it like that."

"It's okay," Kyla said softly. "My thoughts sometimes flash back to that time, too. It was... pretty intense." She hesitated. "And, as much as I try to forget, it's still a part of me."

Jude studied her face. "I hope you keep the happy memories, Kye... somewhere in your heart."

"It's the horrible ones I wish I could erase for good," she said quietly.

"Believe me, Kyla, I've regretted my behaviour that day every day since." He bowed his head. "I'm deeply sorry."

Kyla pushed back her chair. "Let's talk some more, okay? "Come sit on the sofa." She motioned toward the living room and turned up the music slightly. "I know it seems strange, but I don't want Izzy to hear our conversation."

Sitting in the easy chair facing him, Kyla began. "I'm confused, Jude. When you first laid eyes on Izzy, you were in love with her. But the man I knew back then didn't want this." Her voice dropped. "I remember every word you said that day."

Jude leaned forward, clasping his hands together, elbows on his knees. He glanced toward Izzy in her rocker, his expression heavy with thought. "There's a lot you don't know about me," he said finally.

Kyla shifted, crossing her arms as a chill moved through her. The silence stretched long enough that she wasn't sure he would continue.

"Like what?" she asked carefully, trying to steady her voice.

Jude's gaze dropped to the floor.

"Izzy isn't my first child."

Kyla went still.

"Three years ago, my girlfriend got pregnant. We got married and moved into a log house on her parents' property in the Willamette Valley in Oregon." He glanced up briefly. "That's how I got into organic farming."

Kyla nodded once, barely moving, listening.

"We had a beautiful baby boy," Jude continued. "We were both over the moon." His jaw tightened.

"But we lost him."

The words hung in the air.

"He was only two months old."

Kyla moved slowly to the sofa beside him, her presence quiet rather than rushed.

"Oh, Jude... I'm so sorry. What happened?"

"Ever hear of SIDS?" he asked. "Sudden Infant Death Syndrome?"

"Yes," she said softly. "Friends of our family lost their baby that way. Years ago. So sad."

"It was devastating," Jude said, "something I'll never get over."

Kyla glanced toward Izzy, then back to him. "I can't imagine a nightmare like that... especially now that I have—" She corrected herself gently. "We have our beautiful Izzy."

"I blamed myself for a long time," Jude said quietly. "Until I understood it better."

"Why would you blame yourself?"

"Because I was asleep when Chase died."

Kyla's hand found his thigh without thinking, grounding him there. "What do you mean? I don't understand."

"It was a scorching hot summer day," Jude said.

"My wife, Nikki, was shopping in town, and I took Chase into our basement because it was cooler. I brought his bassinet close to the sofa and lay down for a nap."

His voice broke slightly.

"When I woke up... he was blue."

Silence settled hard between them.

Kyla didn't speak at first. The weight of it pressed into the room, leaving no space for anything else.

"I tried artificial respiration," Jude said, his hands curling into fists, "but it felt hopeless. It *was* hopeless."

He turned his face away.

Kyla reached for his shoulder, her touch light. "I'm so sorry."

They sat in silence for a moment.

"I don't know what to say," she whispered at last. "There are just no words for something like that."

"And your wife?" she asked gently.

"Our marriage didn't survive," he said. "In a way... I think Nikki blamed me."

"Many marriages don't survive trauma like that," Kyla said softly. She hesitated. "I'll get us some ice water, okay?"

As Kyla went into the kitchen, the story replayed in her mind in fragmented pieces. By the time she returned, Jude was on the porch. She gave him a moment, then crouched beside Izzy's rocker, watching the steady rise and fall of her chest. She had read everything, followed every recommendation. That was all she could do.

She exhaled quietly.

When she returned, Jude had come back inside.

"Here's some water," she said, handing him a glass.

"I think I understand now... why you said fatherhood wasn't for you. And why you love our daughter so much."

The words *our daughter* still felt unfamiliar, but this time she let them stand.

"And when your marriage ended... is that when you became a traveling organic farmer?"

"Yeah," he said, with a faint, tired laugh. "I needed to get away. That seemed a good way to do it."

"So you've been working at eco-villages for three years?"

"That's right. But I'm getting weary of all the travel." His gaze lifted slightly. "I think it would be good to stay in one place —especially now that I have a good reason to stay on Sunrise."

Kyla studied him carefully. "I'm surprised you came back so soon after the birth."

"I had a few things to figure out," he said. "But once you told me... I couldn't stay away."

She went quiet.

"I remember exactly how you put it," he added. "For the baby's sake, you wanted to avoid a trauma-filled wound that never heals."

His voice softened. "Those were your exact words."

He moved closer, one arm sliding around her shoulders in a steady hold.

"I'm here to help nurture our child. Like any parent, I only want what's best for Izzy."

Kyla didn't pull away.

"Are you thinking of staying here, Jude?" she asked quietly.

"I have a few things to figure out," he said. "But I'd like to live on the island. Sunrise has always drawn me back..., but now I have a much more important reason to stay."

"You're kidding, right, Kye?" Alexa stared at her sister, eyes wide, hands on her hips. Her voice rose, sharp enough to turn heads on the verandah. "I know you asked Jude to connect now and then—whatever his highness could manage, I think you said—but it sounds like he's planning a bigger role than you had in mind."

Kathleen stretched out on the green settee, glancing between the twins, while Jennie cradled Izzy, her grip tightening slightly. It was Saturday, and Alexa had dropped in before her date with Kevin. She visited the family every weekend.

"The fury you unleashed at Jude? Still with me," Kyla said with a half-smile. "And I get how you feel, but I know things now that I didn't know then— and, well... let's just say I understand why Jude behaved the way he did."

"There's no excuse for his behaviour, Kye; I don't care what he told you," Alexa said.

"Um, girls," Jennie said gently, "maybe you'd like to have a private conversation." She gestured toward Kathleen, whose 85th birthday was only a week away.

"Yes, sorry," Kyla said. "I just wanted to tell everyone that Jude may spend more time with us here on the farm."

"He 'may'?" Alexa asked. Then, without waiting: "Nothing like a healthy dose of uncertainty from Mr. Reliable."

Alexa exhaled, running a hand through her hair. "Forget it. I just... I'm worried about you and Izzy, that's all. The last thing you need is my sarcasm."

Kyla smiled, lightly touching Alexa's arm. "No worries, sis. I know a lot of love behind it. Let's just wait and see how things unfold, okay?"

Jennie nodded. "Do you have time for some lunch, Alexa? Mom made sandwiches with cukes from the garden."

"I'll make a pitcher of iced tea," Alexa called over her shoulder as she headed into the house. "Promise I won't overdo the sugar this time."

STARTLED AWAKE by Izzy's piercing cries, Kyla bolted upright, her heart hammering. A tap on the touch-light cast a soft glow across the room as she stumbled toward the bassinet. Her fingers fumbled as she lifted Izzy into her arms.

"Baby, what's wrong?" she whispered, pressing her close. Izzy's skin was hot against her thin pajama top.

The crying sharpened—relentless now. Izzy's face was flushed, her tiny fists clenched as her wails filled the room.

"Shh, it's okay. Mommy's here," Kyla murmured, but it didn't help.

"Where does it hurt, Izzy?" she asked, her voice cracking. She glanced at the clock—3:12 a.m.

Her mind flipped through everything she'd read—pamphlets from the doctor's office, late-night articles, fragments of advice. Gas. Colic. A tight tummhy. Nothing felt certain.

She lay Izzy down and gently lifted her knees to her chest.

The crying didn't ease.

Kyla lifted her again and began pacing, rubbing slow circles on her back.

Nothing worked.

"I don't know what you need," she whispered to the dark.

KYLA BARELY DRAGGED herself out of bed when Izzy cried after 7 a.m.—her usual feeding time. She'd only just fallen into a deep sleep once Izzy finally settled at sunrise. With barely over an hour of rest, she wondered how she'd make it through the day. Then her phone buzzed on the nightstand. Jude's name lit the screen.

"Morning, Sunshine," Jude teased, playing on Kyla's hippie name, Sundance. "Thought I'd check in before starting chores."

"Oh," Kyla sighed heavily. "Just a minute, Jude. "I have to nurse Izzy.—let me put the phone down while I sit with her."

Not waiting for a reply, she set it on the small table by her nursing chair, lifted Izzy from the bassinet, and settled her into position.

"Hi, Jude. Sorry about that. I had maybe about an hour and fifteen minutes of sleep last night. I'm barely functioning."

"Why?" Jude asked. "Something wrong?"

Kyla sank into the cushions and recounted last night's ordeal.

"Sounds like Mama needs some help," he said. "Why don't I sleep over tonight so you don't have to get up?"

Kyla hesitated. The thought of Jude staying overnight hadn't crossed her mind. But she could barely think straight, and the word *help* felt like a gift she didn't quite trust herself to refuse.

"I can't give Izzy my best when I'm running on empty," she reasoned.

"Okay... thanks, Jude. I could use the help."

AT LUNCHTIME, Harry called just as Kyla had stretched out on the sofa with Izzy asleep in the rocker.

"Hey, babe, how's your day?"

Kyla let out a tired laugh. "Feels like it should be night, not day."

"Huh? What do you mean?"

She explained while Harry listened in silence. Then he said, "Hmm... I wish I could help, Kye, but I can't stay over. I need my sleep, too."

Kyla exhaled slowly. "I know, Harry. We all do."

When he finally spoke again, it was, "I can stay over on Saturday if you need me."

Kyla closed her eyes for a moment, Izzy's soft breathing filling the room.

"Hopefully, this is just a one-off for Izzy. But if it keeps up, I'll take you up on that. Thanks, Harry."

AFTER HEARING about Kyla's rough night and Jude's offer to help, Kathleen and Jennie sprang into action.

"We're having pot roast tonight, dear," Kathleen said warmly. "There's plenty for both of you. Why don't I fix up two plates, and maybe Jude can pick them up around six?"

"Better yet," Jennie added, her eyes bright. "Why don't you all come here for dinner? It'd be nice to meet Jude."

Kyla's mind whirled with questions about how this might go. *Is this too soon? Would Jude get the wrong idea—or would they?*

"I picked up the roast from Owen Stewart this morning," Jennie added.

"And we have veggies from our garden, Kye—carrots, potatoes, peas …," Kathleen said.

At the thought of a warm, home-cooked meal, Kyla let out a small breath. Maybe she didn't need to overthink this.

"Thank you both," she said. "I'd love to introduce Jude to you—and I know he'd enjoy meeting you."

Alexa wouldn't be there, she remembered, away at a chiropractic conference in Victoria with Nick and Emily.

AT 5:45, Kyla, Jude, and Izzy stepped into the kitchen, greeted by the rich scent of rosemary, garlic, and onion.

"Oh, that smells amazing, Grandma," Kyla said as Jude shifted to the side, Izzy nestled against his chest.

Kyla introduced Jude to Kathleen, who wiped her hands on her apron before shaking his hand.

"Welcome," she said warmly. "It's lovely to meet you."

"It's great to meet you, too, Kathleen. Thanks so much for having me."

Jennie entered from the dining room, her smile wide. "Hello, you three," she said. Gently brushing Izzy's head, she added, "I'm Kyla's mother, Jennie. I see you have your hands full there, Jude, but please make yourself at home."

"We're just about ready, Kathleen said, giving the gravy a final stir. "Please, take a seat."

As they moved into the dining room, Kyla cleared a space for Izzy's rocker at the end of the long table. Jude set Izzy down carefully, and Kyla buckled the belt snugly around her waist.

"And so, we meet again, Jude," Clay said, stepping off the verandah and extending his hand.

"We do," Jude replied, shaking Clay's hand. "Good to see you again."

"This is my son, Patrick," Clay said as Patrick jogged down the stairs. "Funny how he always knows when dinner's ready," he added with a smile.

"Hi, Jude," Patrick said, nodding. "I hear you're into organic farming."

The conversation around the table flowed easily as they ate.

"I've always wondered what paragliding's like," Jude remarked.

Clay chuckled. "Never tried it? We'll have to fix that. How about Sunday at two? I'll take you up on a tandem ride."

"You can count me in. Anything I need to bring?"

"Just yourself. Meet me at the launch site, and unless the weather shifts, it should be smooth flying."

When Jude learned Patrick had carpentry skills, he said, "If you're interested, I know they need some new fencing at the eco-village. If you want, I can hook you up."

Once they cleared the plates, Kyla stretched, suppressing a yawn. "I hate to eat and run, but I can barely stay awake. Jude offered to take over if Izzy has another crying spell like last night, and I plan to take full advantage."

She smiled at Jude, unbuckled Izzy, and watched as he lifted her from the rocker, cradling her gently.

"Kathleen," Jude said, "that was incredible. I can't thank you enough."

He bounced Izzy lightly and glanced around the table. "I really enjoyed meeting all of you—and, Clay, I'll see you Sunday. Good night, everyone."

~

IN THE COTTAGE, Kyla nursed Izzy and settled her into the bassinet, which she'd moved to the living room. She'd made up the sofa bed for Jude.

Before heading upstairs, she whispered, "I hope you sleep well. Izzy will probably wake up once for a feeding. I'll hear her, don't worry."

"Is there a bottle I can give her instead?" Jude asked. "That way, you can sleep through."

Kyla smiled softly, tilting her head. "That's sweet, but she's never had a bottle. The middle of the night isn't the best time to start."

"Got it," Jude said. "So, you'll come down to nurse her?"

"Yes. I'll know the difference between that cry and last night's. If it's the ordeal, I'll hide my head under the covers and leave you to it." She was half-joking, then added, "If it's too much, call me. I don't expect you to endure hours of crying."

"We'll be fine, Kye. I've got her. Don't worry." Jude brushed a quick kiss over her lips, lingering just a fraction longer than she expected, and she didn't pull away. "Good night," she said, climbing the stairs with a faint smile.

Kyla drifted off soon after, tucking herself under the covers. And when Izzy woke at the witching hour of 3 a.m., she didn't hear a thing.

"Morning!" Kyla called out as she came down the stairs, fully dressed and beaming.

"How lovely to see two of my favourite people on this sunny, blue-sky day," she said in a sing-song voice.

Jude chuckled. "You're a different Kyla than the one I saw yesterday. Amazing what a good sleep will do."

Kyla wrapped her arm around Jude's waist, pulling him close. "Thank you, thank you," she said, pressing a quick kiss to his cheek before gazing at Izzy, sleeping in the bassinet.

"Did she cry at all last night?" Kyla asked. "I didn't hear a thing." She lifted her brows.

"Oh, she cried, all right," Jude replied, "and, as you said—a distinct cry, more like a scream—but I cuddled her, bounced a bit, hummed a tune ..."

"Come on," Kyla said, "You can't tell me it was that easy."

"Where's my trophy?" he teased.

"No, really—what happened?"

Jude grinned. "I paced the kitchen with Izzy until sunrise, wouldn't let her out of my arms. Glad it didn't wake you."

"Oh my gosh," Kyla said, eyes wide. "You're my hero, Jude. Can you stay tonight too? Just kidding."

"I'll come anytime you want me to, Kye," Jude said, his gaze holding hers a touch too long.

Kyla hesitated, for a fraction longer than she meant to, then smiled. "Thanks, Jude. That's good to know." She nudged him playfully. "Pancakes for breakfast? Stewart Owen's homemade sausages on the side?"

"Who's Stewart Owen?" Jude asked.

"Stewart? He's been a Mitchell family friend since before I was born. Has an eye on Kathleen," she said with a laugh.

Jude chuckled. "You know that old saying, 'The way to a man's heart is through his stomach'?

"A saying invented by a man," Kyla teased.

"I'll take a rain check on breakfast. I need to get back to EarthSong and catch a few zees. We're installing a new pond today, and they need my help."

ON SATURDAY EVENING, Harry's white F150 pulled into the turnaround near Kyla's cottage. Rollo barked excitedly, trotting over as Harry stepped out of the truck.

"Rollo, atta boy," Harry called, stepping side-to-side as if to coax him into a game. But at 13, Rollo wasn't interested in games. Harry grinned, scratching behind the dog's ears before heading toward the cottage.

"A sofa bed?" Harry asked, even though its identity was clear. "I figured we'd sleep upstairs, like usual. I can get up when she cries, and you can stay asleep."

Kyla chuckled. "That's not how it works, Harry. The second Izzy cries, I'm awake. If we're all in the same room, you being here doesn't help."

Harry sighed. "Fine. Haven't slept on a pull-out since my ex booted me from our bedroom back in the day."

~

AWAKENED BY IZZY'S CRIES, Kyla came downstairs, already knowing what her daughter needed. As she passed the sofa bed, she saw that Harry's eyes were closed.

Some help, she thought with a smirk. When he rolled over, she wondered if he was really asleep—or just pretending to ignore the baby's cries.

After nursing Izzy, Kyla returned upstairs and didn't hear another sound for the rest of the night. But by morning, her daughter's cries echoed through the cottage.

When Kyla reached the main floor, she found Harry bouncing Izzy up and down with more enthusiasm than finesse. *Does he really think that's helping?*

"I'm glad you're here, Kye," Harry said, quickly passing the baby to her.

"Aw, come here, baby," Kyla murmured, realizing a diaper change was in order.

"Harry, you know how to change her," she said. "I've shown you, and you've seen me do it plenty of times."

How long would he have waited if I hadn't come down?

She glanced at him—hair tousled, shirt wrinkled—and a new thought crept in.

Please don't tell me he's one of those men who won't change a diaper.

ON SUNDAY AT TWO, Jude met Clay at the paragliding launch site. It was another hot day... but a steady breeze stirred the air —enough for a clean launch.

Everything went smoothly, and as they landed back on the clifftop, Clay packed up his equipment while Jude grinned, still riding the adrenaline. "Clay, that was exhilarating. And the birds-eye view... incredible from up there."

Clay nodded. "If you ever want to take up the sport, I recommend lessons from a pro. Like anything, there are clowns out there who put themselves—and everyone else—at risk."

Jude laughed. "I'd love to, but I have a few things to handle first. Need help with that?"

"Nah, I store it over there," Clay said, motioning to a nearby storage shed. "Part of the routine."

"Thanks again, Clay. That was incredible." As Jude started across the field toward his bike, movement near the cottager caught his eye. Kyla and Harry stepped out of the cottage, the baby snug against Harry's chest with a sunhat tilted slightly askew. "Jude," Kyla called, "I didn't know you were here."

"Yeah, just had the most amazing tandem ride with Clay," Jude replied.

Their paths met near the cottage, and they stopped to chat.

Jude gently straightened Izzy's hat and murmured, "There you go, sweetie."

Harry shifted, drawing Izzy a little closer across his chest. "We should get going, Kye. The fishing boat leaves at five."

"After some fresh salmon?" Jude asked, glancing at Harry.

"Yep," Harry replied, already turning toward the truck. "Have a good week, Jude," he added over his shoulder.

THE FOLLOWING SATURDAY EVENING, Kyla dressed Izzy in her ivory sleep sack and placed her on her back in the bassinet. "Nighty-night, sweet baby girl," Kyla whispered, gently brushing her thumb across the baby's forehead.

As she descended the stairs, she glanced at Harry scrolling through his phone. She set the baby monitor on a side table and glanced at it, smiling at Izzy in that adorable pose—both arms raised over her head.

She waited for Harry so they could resume their visit away from screens. He'd be staying overnight since tomorrow wasn't a workday. Even so, she valued times when she could feel more like a lover than a mom, but Harry barely looked up.

Kyla fidgeted with her hands as Harry continued to scroll. When her phone chimed, and Jude's name flashed across the screen, she read his text.

"Hey, Harry's truck is in the yard—I won't bother you."

Kyla texted, "It's all right, Jude. Where are you?"

"I'm right outside your cottage. Couldn't pass by without saying hello."

"Had another amazing tandem ride with Clay. Heading back to EarthSong now."

"That's—" Kyla stopped texting when she heard Izzy coughing over the monitor. Within moments, the cough intensified, causing Kyla to race upstairs to her side. By now, Izzy's breathing was turning labored, and panic crept over Kyla. She was vaguely aware of Harry entering the room, hovering near the doorway, as if unsure of what to do.

When communication stopped abruptly, and Jude heard a commotion inside the house, he rushed to the front door and pushed it open without knocking.

"Kyla," he shouted, "is something wrong?"

Not waiting for an answer, he charged upstairs, stopping to assess the situation. He gently but firmly lifted the baby and took her into his arms. Turning her over, supporting her along his forearm, Jude gently patted her back to help her breathe.

"It's okay, baby; it's okay. You're going to be all right," he said softly, remaining calm.

"She's probably okay," Harry said, his voice uncertain. "Babies cough, right?" But even as he spoke, he stayed rooted near the door, as if waiting for them to handle it.

As Jude held Izzy, his calm presence helped put Kyla at ease. Harry's voice faded into the background beside the steady calm Jude brought into the room. *How had she ever questioned him?*

When Izzy kept coughing, Jude said, "We need to get to the hospital, Kye. If you drive, I'll stay with Izzy in case I need to give her CPR."

Kyla's heart raced as she grabbed her keys and a baby blanket.

Harry shifted in the doorway, arms folded. "She's tough, Kye. Maybe give it a minute?"

As if Harry hadn't spoken, Jude rushed to Kyla's Forrester, opened the back door, and resumed patting Izzy's back.

"I'll drive, Kyla," Harry said, reaching for her keys.

Kyla sat in the back, every muscle tight.

"Kye, call ahead to Lady Minto and let them know we'll be there in about five minutes," Jude said. "Tell them what's happening."

~

AFTER IZZY WAS STABLE, Kyla sat beside Jude in her hospital room.

Harry had gone to the cafeteria, hoping to find a machine where he could buy something to eat.

Kyla watched Jude as he held their baby, rocking her gently until she fell back to sleep. She'd thought love was about passion and shared laughs, but watching Jude cradle Izzy now, she realized it could be this, too—a quiet, unwavering presence in the middle of the storm. The ease with which he handled Izzy, the steady warmth in his touch, and his instinct in a crisis shifted something in her.

Kyla reached out, her fingers brushing over Jude's as he passed Izzy to her. His hand lingered longer than necessary, and that was enough for her.

~

"SORRY, can't make it for dinner tonight, Kye."

Harry's text surprised Kyla, but not unpleasantly. She'd been staring at the empty fridge, debating whether to raid her grandmother's freezer—never her first choice. Grandma always has something frozen for emergencies, she thought, smirking.

"Signed up for a tennis tournament, and forgot it's tonight. Apologies."

Kyla noticed he hadn't suggested a rain check.

"No worries, Harry. Knock 'em dead with your overhead smash," she wrote, remembering his signature move.

"I saw Harry at the café on Saturday," Alexa mentioned during her visit. "He and his friends were off to the Discovery Islands for kayaking."

Kyla blinked. "Oh, I love kayaking. Feels like forever since we did that."

Alexa arched a brow. "Harry usually stays over on Saturdays, doesn't he?

Kyla scrolled her phone messages. "Yeah, and I don't remember getting a text from him ..."

"But, he's the reliable one," Alexa remarked, her forehead furrowed.

"Lex, you know things have moved in a different direction," Kyla said softly. "Harry's been amazing—supportive in his way. But he's trying to fit into a role that doesn't come naturally. And I get it. I'm still figuring this out, too."

Alexa didn't let it go. "He's a vet, Kye. Stable. Dependable. You've known him for six years."

Kyla exhaled, shrugging. "Yeah. And I've learned Harry's great... when it fits his schedule. Fatherhood's optional for him. For Jude..." Her voice softened, "It isn't. It's instinctive. The way he is with Izzy... he just clicks with her."

Alexa crossed her arms. "You remember Jude backed out the second you told him, right?

"I do." Kyla locked eyes with Alexa. "But people grow, Lex. Harry is thirty-one; Jude is only twenty-three. And Jude is showing up now. I can't ignore that."

Alexa's features softened as she squeezed Kyla's shoulder. "Fair enough. Just don't hurt Harry if it comes to that. He's a good guy.'

"I know. I care about him—but Izzy's my focus. Jude feels like the right path for her."

Kyla's phone chimed. She read aloud:

"Having a blast kayaking. Thought of all our old trips. I won't make it back tonight. Next Saturday, for sure?"

Kyla's thumbs hovered before typing. 'Take care, Harry. Next Saturday works. Have fun."

Alexa watched her closely. "He's pulling away."

Kyla smiled faintly. "Yeah. And I think that's okay."

HARRY ARRIVED right on time the next Saturday. Stepping into the cottage, he set a bottle of Bordeaux on the kitchen counter and brushed a quick kiss over Kyla's lips.

Izzy rested in her rocker on the kitchen table. "Hey, sweet girl" Harry said, "I missed you. Maybe we can all go kayaking someday."

He sniffed the air. "Something smells good in here. Anything I can do to help?"

"Maybe just crack open that red wine while I serve the pizza," Kyla said, slipping on oven mitts. "I thought we could eat outside and watch the sunset—what do you think?"

"Sounds great." Harry picked up the bottle. "I'll bring the wine and glasses outside. I saw you'd set up a table."

"Do you mind taking Izzy out, too? We can put her rocker on the porch floor so she can see us, but it won't take up table space."

AFTER A DELIGHTFUL EVENING beneath a stunning summer sunset, they cleared the table and brought Izzy inside. Just as Harry set her down on the kitchen table, his phone buzzed.

"Mind if I get this, Kye?"

"Of course not," she said easily.

"Kevin, hi—what's up, man?"

Izzy cried, and Harry stepped back out onto the porch to finish his call. When he returned, Kyla was nursing Izzy.

She smiled at him, waiting for him to pick up the thread of his conversation. *Any moment now,* she thought. He's about to be called away again.

"That was Kevin—Alexa's boyfriend. The dentist, you know?"

"Oh, yes," Kyla said. "If I'm not mistaken, you two met at the Mitchell family Christmas Open House, right?"

"Yeah. We've been hanging out a bit," Harry said. "He was at the kayaking trip last weekend."

Kyla warmed at that, glad he was making friends. *It doesn't matter,* she told herself. *It's more important that he's happy than anything else.*

"Anyway..." Harry glanced down. "Would I be in your bad books again if I bowed out of the overnight stay?"

Kyla blinked. "Not at all, Harry. I've enjoyed tonight. What's up?"

"Kevin invited a few guys to play poker. One of them dropped out, and he asked me if I wanted to fill in."

"Sounds good. I'm glad you're socializing more—it's good for you."

"I'll be around," Harry said, gathering his things. He kissed the top of Izzy's head, then brushed a quick kiss against Kyla's cheek before heading out.

As the door closed, the house settled into quiet—lighter, somehow.

Kyla couldn't explain it, but she didn't resist it.

"I CAN'T STAY TOO late tonight," Jude said, stacking plates by the sink. "I've got an early call with the ministry tomorrow."

Kyla glanced over. "Forests?"

"Yeah—Ministry of Forests. Mostly remote work, but I'll head into Victoria now and then." He shrugged, but she caught the twitch in the corner of his mouth.

"Jude." She set down the dish towel and crossed her arms. "You got a job with the Ministry of Forests and didn't think to mention it?"

A grin spread across his face. "It wasn't official until last week. I didn't want to jinx it."

Kyla stepped into him and wrapped her arms tightly around his waist. "I'm so proud of you," she murmured, her voice catching.

When she pulled back, her eyes were bright. She looked at him for a long moment, as if trying to take it in all at once.

"This is good," she said softly. "For you. For us."

KYLA LEANED AGAINST THE RAILING, watching Jennie and Clay make their way toward the clifftop, their fingers intertwined. There was an ease to the way they moved together—like they'd done it a thousand times, their steps effortlessly in sync.

It reminded her of Jennie and her dad, Derrick, when she was a child—the way they'd lock eyes as if no one else existed. She had always admired that kind of bond: steady, unshakable, built quietly over time.

She wondered if she and Jude could grow into something like that.

Their relationship wasn't struggling, but it was still new, still untested. And yet, watching Jennie and Clay, something in her softened.

Maybe it wouldn't happen quickly. But if they kept choosing each other—kept showing up, even on the ordinary days—perhaps one day they would move like that too, without thinking, without effort.

Around the island, she'd seen couples like that before: people who had lasted. She'd always found something reassuring in it.

And for the first time, she let herself imagine she and Jude might be on their way there.

2

NICK

January, 2024

Nick chained his bicycle to the rack outside the office space he rented in Grace Square. The steel bit into his bare fingers as he wrapped the chain around the post. Through the clinic window, he noticed two of the six waiting room chairs occupied—a sign of his growing practice.

After greeting his patients and Ginny, the receptionist, Nick settled into his private office and reviewed his schedule. He ran a hand through his hair. The patient list was full, but one name stood out—Stewart. The Mitchell family's dear friend had been coming to the clinic since day one, but lately, Nick had noticed him moving more slowly, wincing more. Today, he would find a way to bring it up without Stewart brushing it off.

"As soon as Stewart arrives," Nick said to Ginny, "send him to Treatment Room One, please."

Stewart shuffled inside, his steps more laboured than before.

"Morning, Doc," Stewart said, lowering himself onto the chair across from Nick's desk, a quiet groan escaping him.

Nick smiled. "Morning, Stewart. How's the arthritis treating you?"

Stewart waved a hand. "Same as always. Stiff, slow. But nothing I can't handle."

Nick nodded but didn't push. He'd bring it up again after the exam.

As he worked through Stewart's treatments, Nick's mind wandered. Left to his own devices, Stewart would keep toughing it out—but he needed help, and Nick knew just the person: Charlotte. She'd been looking for work, and Stewart needed someone to temper his tendency to work too hard.

When they finished, Nick leaned against his desk. "Stewart, have you ever thought about getting some extra help around the house? Just a few hours a week."

Stewart scoffed. "I may have slowed down, Nick, but I'm perfectly capable of managing on my own, thanks."

"It's not about that," Nick said carefully. "Just someone to help with housecleaning, laundry... maybe even some gardening. I know someone who's looking for work—Charlotte. She's reliable, and she'll respect your privacy."

Stewart eyed him. "Charlotte, huh? She's Emily's mom, right?"

"That's her. Everyone calls her Lottie."

When Stewart didn't respond, Nick added, "No pressure—just think about it."

Stewart didn't say no, and Nick counted it as a small victory.

As Nick completed his treatment notes, he paused at the screen. Stewart had been his very first patient. A familiar ache settled in. For a moment, he could almost see his dad, Derrick, in the doorway, offering a proud grin and a thumbs-up—just as he had so many times.

But that day never came. Derrick was gone long before Nick graduated, before the clinic was more than a rough sketch in the corner of his notebook.

Still, Stewart had made sure Nick didn't face an empty waiting room that first morning, booking the first appointment himself. In some ways, it felt like Derrick had sent him.

NOW THAT CHARLOTTE had moved from England to Sunrise Island, away from her estranged husband, the Mitchell family —and Bev in particular—were finding ways to help her settle in. No one expected Charlotte to leave Sunrise Island, but she knew she needed to find work to support herself.

Nick felt a pang of sadness watching Stewart hobble out of the treatment room toward the reception desk. Poking his head into Treatment Room Two, he checked in with his next patient.

"I'll only be a moment, Peg, and then we can do your gait scan, okay?"

"No rush, Dr. Nick. I'll catch up on my emails," she replied, already scrolling through her phone.

As Stewart turned to leave, Nick called after him. "Stewart, let's have a word. I'll follow you to your truck."

Just as they stepped outside, Emily appeared on the sidewalk, about to enter the clinic.

"Em," Nick said, his face lighting up with a smile. "You're early. Mind doing Peggy's gait scan while I chat with Stewart?"

"Happy to," Emily replied, heading toward the gait scanner."

Nick stood beside Stewart's black pickup. Stewart chuckled. "So, you think I'm ready for the boneyard, do you?"

"Not at all. Nowhere near," Nick said with a grin. "But I've got an idea that might interest you."

Stewart hesitated. "Oh, uh... not sure, to tell you the truth, Nick..."

Nick smiled knowingly. "Kathleen would love to have you and Lottie over for dinner on Sunday. What do you say?"

Stewart's expression softened. "You know me too well. If Kathleen's up for it, I'll be there."

Nick laughed. "Lottie was already coming, so one more plate won't make a difference."

"It's a date, then," Stewart replied with a nod. "The usual time, I assume."

"Six o'clock sharp," Nick said with a laugh. "We can't keep Commander Kathleen waiting."

Shifting his truck into reverse, Stewart smiled. "I'll look forward to it. And thanks, Nick."

Nick watched Stewart's truck pull out, the tailpipe puffing soft clouds of exhaust into the crisp winter air. He tucked his hands into his coat pockets, gazing toward the horizon where the sea stretched beyond Grace Square's rooftops. Sunrise Island had a way of holding on to people—rooting them deeper even when they thought they might drift away.

His thoughts drifted to Emily. Since Charlotte's arrival, she'd been spending more time at the clinic, often staying late to review patient files, study imaging, and co-manage cases with the medical doctor. While she'd been content with part-time hours to help her mother, she now felt free to focus more fully on her practice.

As Nick stepped inside the clinic, Ginny glanced up from her desk.

"Emily's in Treatment Room Two," she said with a grin. "Already stealing your patients."

"Nah," Nick said, shaking his head. "Most of our patients are happy to see either of us. That flexibility helps with scheduling, you'll see, Ginny."

"But I'm sure some men prefer you, Dr. Nick," Ginny replied, "just as the ladies seem to book with Dr. Emily."

Nick paused at Ginny's words and approached the reception desk. Resting his elbows on the higher part of the counter, he said, "Let me clear something up. Many people think chiropractic adjustments need to be forceful—'If it doesn't hurt, it's not working'. That's not the case."

He stopped for a moment, checking to see if Ginny was listening. "The chiropractic adjustment is concerned with line of drive and line of correction, not brute force," he explained, noticing Ginny's distracted look.

Realizing his mistake, Nick back-pedalled. "Sorry, Ginny; I got carried away there. I'll explain more later, and attending the educational seminars with Em and me will help you better understand the science behind our profession," he said, pushing himself away from the desk and heading toward Treatment Room Two.

He found Emily gently tractioning Peggy's right foot. Peggy tucked her auburn hair into a loose bun, leaving a few stray curls to frame her face. "Oh, that feels good," Peggy said. "Can I bring you home with me?"

Emily laughed softly at a question she'd heard many times. "I think you'll find a difference with orthotics, Peg."

Emily lowered the table, helping Peggy get up. "There you go. We'll call when they come in... should only be a couple of weeks."

Peggy patted Emily's hand. "You're a gem, dear. Nick's lucky to have you here."

Nick leaned casually against the doorframe. "I'd say so."

As Nick moved aside, Peggy made her way to the front desk, leaving them alone.

Nick crossed the room, slipping his arms around Emily's waist. "You know," he murmured, "you've been spending more time here than ever, babe, and it feels like how I envisioned building our practice together—the way we'd planned."

Emily leaned into him, her cheek nestled into his shoulder. "I've been thinking about that," she said. "I'm finally ready to focus on the clinic."

Nick's heart quickened as he realized how much they'd

built together, both professionally and personally. He pulled back just enough to meet her gaze. "Are you saying you're ready to go full-time?"

She nodded. "Charlotte's settled in. She even mentioned joining that garden club Kathleen's been raving about."

Nick kissed her temple gently. "Maybe it's time we start planning—not just for the clinic, but for our future together."

Emily's eyes softened. "I'd like that."

"How 'bout I make a reservation at the Driftwood Inn for Friday at six?"

"Mmm, sounds romantic, Doctor," Emily said. Her eyes shifted to the computer screen. "My eleven o'clock patient is here, so… until next time, my dearest."

THE DRIFTWOOD INN exuded an enduring charm—soft candlelight, the gentle hum of conversation, and the occasional crackle from the fireplace. Nick sat across from Emily, his heart doing that ridiculous flutter it hadn't done since he was a teenager.

She was radiant tonight, he thought, the soft waves of her hair catching the candlelight as she laughed at something he'd said—though Nick couldn't recall what it was. He couldn't stop glancing toward the entrance, anticipating the bouquet.

Nick's gaze lingered on Emily as she skimmed the menu. She seemed blissfully unaware of the tension building inside him.

"I think I'll go with the halibut," she said. "What about you?"

"Salmon," Nick replied, barely hearing his voice.

Emily's eyes narrowed slightly. "You okay?" she asked.

"Yeah," he said, smiling, trying to hide his nervousness. "Just thinking how glad I am you're here."

Remembering the first time he proposed, last Christmas, he'd been sure it would mark the beginning of their future together—until she'd walked away.

Tonight felt different.

Emily reached across the table, threading her fingers through his. "Me too."

Movement by the entrance caught Nick's attention. He straightened as Clay and the others—Jennie, Alexa, Kyla, and Charlotte—filed in and took a table across from them.

Emily's face lit up. "Oh! I didn't know you'd be here tonight," she called over. "How great you're so close by."

"No kidding," Alexa said, casting a knowing glance at Nick that he pretended not to notice.

Jennie grinned. "Felt like a good night for seafood."

"Mom, I know those scallops have your name on them," Nick teased.

Jennie laughed softly. "Noted," she said. "Hard to resist."

As the server took Emily and Nick's orders, and slipped toward the family's table, Emily leaned in, her gaze searching Nick's face.

"You're quiet tonight."

Nick hesitated, his fingers tracing the stem of his glass. "I was thinking... maybe we could plan a trip to the Bahamas next summer to celebrate our first year in practice."

Emily's eyes sparkled. "That sounds perfect—if we can swing it. White sands and blue skies sound pretty amazing right now," she mused, glancing toward the fire.

Before Nick could respond, a server appeared and set down a bountiful bouquet of white roses laced with eucalyptus. Emily gasped, touching the petals lightly.

"What's this?" She leaned closer, noticing a small box nestled in a gauze pouch, secured to the vase with a white silk ribbon.

The server returned with a silver champagne bucket, set it

beside them, and poured two glasses. A hush settled over the room, curiosity rippling toward their table.

The musicians shifted seamlessly into "I Will".

Nick rose, heart hammering in his chest as he untied the ribbon and cradled the box in his palm.

Emily stilled, her hand rising to her lips.

Nick took a steadying breath. This time, he wouldn't lose her.

"Em... I've loved you from the day you walked into that first class and turned my life upside down. I can't imagine life without you."

His thumb brushed over the box as he opened it. "Will you marry me?"

Tears spilled over as Emily nodded, a laugh breaking through her tears. "Yes. Yes—of course, yes!"

Applause erupted around them as Nick slid the ring onto her finger. Emily pulled him into a kiss, as if the room had disappeared altogether.

Jennie was first to her feet, drawing Emily into a hug. "We couldn't be happier," she whispered, blinking back tears.

"To Nick and Emily," Clay toasted, lifting his glass. The others followed, their glasses catching the candlelight.

Later, as the plates cleared and conversation softened, Nick reached for Emily's hands.

"You were worth the wait," he murmured, brushing his lips over her engagement ring.

Emily traced slow circles over his hand. "And you... you're home to me." Her smile carried a quiet certainty. "How does July sound?"

Nick squeezed her hands gently, his heart full. "July sounds perfect."

～

On Saturday morning, Nick and Emily lay in bed, warm under the covers, while the crisp January air frosted the hexagonal window with delicate designs like white lace.

"Em," Nick began, "how would you feel if..."

"I know what you're about to say," Emily said with a giggle, rolling onto her side to face him. "You want to get married here, on the Mitchell farm."

Nick smirked. "Is it that obvious?"

"I was going to suggest it myself," Emily replied, her smile softening. And I wouldn't have it any other way. I've been here long enough to understand your family history—and what this place means to people."

Nick's smile widened. "And you're part of that now," he said, wrapping an arm around her and drawing her close.

"Your Christmas Open House, the island markets, the sense of community... it all feels like Sunrise," Emily said. "I can already picture how much a wedding here would mean—not just to us, but to everyone who's been part of your life."

Nick nodded, his gaze tender. "Exactly. We mark the big moments here. Even my dad's funeral felt like a community tribute. After breakfast, I'll show you where Mom scattered his ashes. Then we can walk the property and find the perfect spot for the wedding."

Nick took Emily to the clifftop where Jennie had stood, scattering Derrick's ashes. "It was a sad day, but it's comforting to come here whenever we want. It brings me peace."

Emily reached for his hand. "I can understand that, honey. And I love the idea of choosing a wedding site we can visit every year on our anniversary," she said tenderly.

As they headed toward the corral, Rollo caught up with them, his tail wagging happily until a squirrel darted past and he lumbered off in pursuit, though he didn't stand a chance of catching it anyway.

"Rollo has slowed down," Nick remarked. "He's been with us for about thirteen years now."

Emily smiled. "He was so cute in his Santa hat, sitting in the Christmas sleigh."

They strolled past the fruit orchard, still hand-in-hand. Nick kicked a pine cone as they approached the site where his ancestors had first settled on the Mitchell property. "See this here, Em? My grandfather moved the two original cottages from this spot closer to the farmhouse. Kyla and Patrick live in them now."

"How cool is that?" Emily said, her eyes lighting up. "I'd love to learn more about your family history."

Nick laughed. "Grandma would love to tell you everything —but I warn you, you'll be stuck for at least a week, maybe longer."

As he spoke, a glint of silver caught his eye. Letting go of Emily's hand, he walked over and crouched down, brushing the dirt off a half-buried object. It was a jackknife, tarnished with age. He wiped it clean on the hem of his shirt, revealing an insignia etched into the handle.

"What is it?" Emily asked, noticing the change in his expression.

Nick stared at the knife, his voice soft. "This must've been Dad's. From his college days, I think." He tried to open it, but the blade jammed.

Emily knelt beside him. "Maybe this is the spot, Nick. For the wedding, I mean. The history, the view—and now finding your dad's jackknife here—it feels like a sign."

Nick stood, slipping the knife into his pocket. He looked around, taking in the sweeping view. After a moment, he nodded. "One of the best spots on the property," he said. "I think we've made our choice."

Their arms wrapped around each other, and they kissed deeply, full of warmth and quiet joy. When they pulled apart, Emily's eyes sparkled with an idea. "What do you think about getting a gazebo—one of those white, wedding cake-like ones?"

Nick laughed. "I'm sure we can figure something out. But if you know this family, you know we like to do things ourselves. Patrick's a carpenter; let's talk to him and see what he can build for us."

~

"Can you find me a picture so I know exactly what you have in mind, Em?" Patrick's Irish blue eyes caught the light, the shade even brighter against his blue shirt.

Emily reached for her phone and opened Notes, where she'd saved a photo of a gazebo she'd visited at an up-island resort. "Here," she said, holding up the phone. "Something like this?"

Patrick studied the photo. The black-shingled roof had three tiers; the rest was all in white, with decorative scalloped edges and corner supports on each of the ten posts—intricate work only a skilled artisan could achieve."

"Yep," Patrick said, his brow furrowed. "That'd do the trick, all right. But for the cost of making that, you'd be better off buying one. Have it delivered here."

"Oh, okay then, Patrick," Nick said. "We'll research it. Thanks for checking it out, though," he added, patting Patrick on the back. "Oh, by the way, if Stewart and Lottie agree about her working at his place, is there a chance you might build a place for her to live... on his property?"

"Not sure, man; I'd have to see his place first, but aren't you getting ahead of yourself?"

"What, me?" Nick said with a laugh. "I guess I'm guilty of putting the cart before the horse sometimes."

"Let's look at the facts," Emily said. "Lottie doesn't realize we're plotting and scheming a way to help both her and Stewart, and all Stewart knows is that we think it might be a good idea for him to hire Lottie to help with the chores. Lottie's aware that people are trying to find ways for her to support herself... that's it. Let's wait and see how things go over dinner tonight, shall we?"

THE FAMILY GATHERED on the Mitchell farmhouse porch as the late afternoon sunlight filtered through the trees, casting a golden glow across the fields. Warmed by heat lamps and the soft light of hurricane lamps, the scene felt typical, even in winter. Lottie was in the kitchen, helping with dinner preparations, while Kathleen lingered on the verandah, eager to hear how the conversation would unfold.

Stewart sat in his usual spot—a sturdy rocking chair that creaked softly as he leaned back. His hands, knotted from years of hard work and arthritis, rested on the armrests. He surveyed the group with a sharp gaze, his independence a badge of pride he wore as plainly as the flannel shirt on his back.

Nick cleared his throat, glancing at Emily for reassurance before speaking. "Stewart, about that idea we discussed..."

Stewart's eyes narrowed. "I've done fine on my own for almost thirty years. Why would I need someone now?"

Kathleen, seated nearby, leaned forward slightly. Her voice was gentle but firm, with a tone that only years of wisdom could shape. "Stewart, no one's questioning your ability. But arthritis is a hard taskmaster, and there's no shame in letting someone lend a hand. Lottie's got energy to spare, and she could really use the work. It's a win-win in my opinion."

Stewart hesitated, his fingers drumming against the

armrest. "I don't know. I like my privacy. Having someone underfoot all the time isn't exactly my idea of peaceful living."

"That's fair," Emily chimed in. "But what if we made it so she had her own space? Patrick could help build a small cottage or studio on the property if you're open to it. She'd have her independence, and you'd still have your privacy. It could work out well for both of you."

Patrick nodded, his blue eyes thoughtful. "I'd be happy to take on the project, Stewart. We could design it together—make sure it fits the property and gives Lottie a place she'll love. Something practical, but cozy."

Stewart looked out over the fields, his jaw tightening. The silence stretched, but no one interrupted, giving him space to process the idea. Finally, he exhaled a long breath, his gaze softening. "I suppose it's worth considering," he said grudgingly. "As long as it's done right—and as long as Lottie's okay with it."

Kathleen smiled warmly. "I think you'll find she'll be more than okay with it. When we visited your roadside stand on Thursday, she admired your place. She even said something like, 'Now, if I had the money, I'd run a farm like this.'"

Stewart's lips quirked in a small smile. "Well, I can't argue with good taste—so long as she doesn't try to tell me what to do."

Patrick grinned. "I'll make sure it's a place she'll love—and you'll still have all the space you need."

As the family relaxed, the conversation shifted to plans for the coming week, but the glimmer of hope lingered in the air. Stewart may have resisted at first, but they could all see the walls he'd built around his independence beginning to crack—just enough to let in a little light.

"Now," Kathleen said, "dinner's ready. After we eat, how about we give you and Lottie some time alone and see if you can work something out?"

"Okay, Kathleen; if you think it's a good idea, then I'm sold," he said, squeezing her arm as he passed by.

It was Kathleen's custom to invite everyone for dinner on Sundays whenever possible. Tonight, Clay, Jennie, Kyla, Izzy, Jude, Alexa, Lottie, and Stewart gathered around the red oak dining table. "Sunday roasts are easy," she'd claimed, "and Stewart's are the best."

When everyone finished, squeezing into the room for chocolate cake, even with stomachs already bursting, they shifted away from the table. "Stewart... Lottie," Jennie said, calling them toward her. "You're welcome to chat in the home office," she said, gesturing toward the open door. It would be more private in there," she said with a smile.

"Sounds serious," Stewart joked, motioning for Lottie to go ahead of him.

After they shut the door, laughter erupted from the office. The laughter was contagious, and soon it echoed throughout the house.

When Lottie finally swung open the door, she announced to anyone listening, "We've agreed. You can call me Charlotte Warren, Personal Assistant to Mr. Stewart Owen of Cedargrove Farms."

Stewart linked arms with Lottie. "Maybe you can help me find my keys," he said, "and I'll pick you up at ten tomorrow. Patrick, can you come along with us?"

"I can drive over with Lottie if Dad will lend me his F150," Patrick said, glancing at Clay.

"I'm working here tomorrow, Patrick, so it's all yours."

3

———

ALEXA

"**B**lackcomb's my favourite mountain," Alexa declared as her skis glided to a stop beside Kevin's at the base of the hill. They had lingered at the summit, drinking hot chocolate in Horstman Hut until just before closing. With no one else in sight, their ski-out to the base had been uninterrupted, thrilling, and utterly theirs.

"You skied down that mountain like a champion," Alexa remarked, a playful lilt in her voice.

"My technique is flawless," Kevin replied, without cracking a smile.

Alexa waited for the follow-up—maybe something about how he'd been skiing since the age of four, *he learned from the best...* but none came. Humility is not his strong suit, she thought to herself. That's for sure.

Returning to their rented condo, they changed into bathing suits and made their way to the hot tub. Settling in among the other guests, they raised chilled glasses of chardonnay. The steaming water was a welcome contrast to the crisp night air.

As the first snowflakes drifted down, Alexa tilted her head back, marvelling at the flurries gathering in the night sky. "Let's stay here forever, Kev. Just like this," she murmured. She closed her eyes and opened her mouth to catch a snowflake.

Kevin chuckled, brushing a stray flake from her cheek before leaning in. He sealed his lips over hers, warm and soft. For a moment, the world fell away—the soft fall of snow, the surrounding chatter, everything. It was just the two of them, alone together, beneath the winter sky.

~

ON THE WAY HOME, Kevin couldn't stop planning their next adventure.

"How about skydiving, Lex?"

"No, thanks," Alexa replied, shaking her head. "I like my life too much."

Kevin grinned. "It's one of the most exhilarating things I've ever done."

"Everyone gets worked up about pulling the chute in time, but not me." He stole a glance at her instead of the snowy road ahead. "I nailed it. No panic, no hesitation. It's all about trusting your instincts."

As he launched into a detailed play-by-play, painting himself as the star of the dive, Alexa listened with a mix of amusement and exasperation. His enthusiasm was infectious, even if he had a way of turning every story into his highlight reel. Still, she loved how alive he became when sharing his experiences and marvelled at the fact that she was still dating her longtime crush.

Alexa playfully rolled her eyes, glancing at Emily, and they both turned away, not wanting to offend Kevin.

Back home, the conversation shifted to tennis. Kevin convinced Nick and Emily to sign up for a doubles program at the rec center. The four-week session included refresher lessons, which Emily was quick to embrace.

"I'm in," Emily said, smiling. "It's been forever since I've played."

Kevin shrugged. "The lessons bore me, but once we're past that..."

Alexa playfully rolled her eyes, exchanging a glance with Emily. They both turned away to stifle their laughter, not wanting to bruise Kevin's ego.

As the first session got underway, Alexa noticed how much Nick and Emily enjoyed themselves. They moved across the court with ease, their laughter echoing as they rallied. Alexa, ever the competitive one, poured her energy into the game, determined to keep up.

"Good job, guys!" she called after losing a game.

Kevin raised a brow. "We're not playing golf here, Lexi," he teased when she sent the ball soaring into the air with an awkward scoop of her racket.

"Careful, Kev," Nick chimed in with a grin. "She's not just your tennis partner—she's your neighbor."

Alexa laughed, despite a small twinge of annoyance at Kevin's comment. He could be charming, sure, but sometimes his casual jabs struck a nerve, especially when she was trying her best. Still, a quiet thought lingered—she wasn't as good as Keven at this. Not yet, anyway.

ON THEIR MAY kayaking trip to the Discovery Islands, Alexa saw a different side of her boyfriend.

Even though they'd paddled these waters before, they knew conditions could change quickly. Before setting out, they checked the wind and currents, planning to reassess as they went. Alexa considered herself an intermediate paddler, while Kevin's more advanced skills gave her confidence.

Kevin made sure they had everything they needed: signal

flares, a VHF radio, a satellite messenger, and fully charged cell phones in waterproof cases tethered to their kayaks. They left their float plan with their colleague at the dental clinic.

After taking the ferry from Sunrise to Victoria, they launched from Oak Bay Marina—a shorter route, but one known for stronger currents. The early morning crossing was peaceful, the water calm beneath a friendly sky and light wind. Dressed in matching red flotation jackets, they paddled in sync in the double kayak, Alexa seated behind Kevin, enjoying the rhythm while staying alert for any change in conditions.

Spotting an opening in the breakwater, they moved ahead, watching carefully for other boaters. The Chain Islands came into view, with Harris Island offering a good place to pause, assess conditions, and check boat traffic before continuing toward Great Chain Island.

The water grew rougher, and Alexa felt a smidgeon of doubt about handling the stronger currents.

"Could be a little rough crossing Mayor Channel," Kevin warned. "We might have to ferry glide."

After checking the current, he adjusted their angle, and they aimed for Great Chain Island.

Navigating through the Great Chain Islets, an ecological reserve, they observed harbor seals sunning on exposed rocks, a colony of sea lions, and black oystercatchers—their shrill cries and bright orange beaks making them easy to spot.

Drawn in by the quiet, they drifted ashore along a stony beach for a short break. Laughing, they straddled driftwood logs, soaking up the rugged beauty of Discovery before pushing off again.

As currents swirled, they chose a route through the islets leading to Discovery Island. After checking the winds in Plumper Passage, Kevin determined it was safe to cross.

"We'll ferry glide across the channel, Lexi," he said, angling the kayak slightly. "By paddling at an angle to the current instead of fighting it head-on, we can stay in control and hold our position."

They reached slower waters and eddies near the shoreline, where a cluster of driftwood logs had gathered. Kevin guided them in for a quick pause, and they straddled one just long enough to stretch their legs and reset before pushing off again.

"We'll head south along the shore and around Commodore Point," Kevin shouted, "to Rudlin Bay. We can land there and have lunch."

"Yay," Alexa said, her stomach rumbling. "It's time for a break."

The coarse sand and pebbled beach at Rudlin Bay, sheltered from the waves, offered a perfect place to land. Kevin pulled the kayak onto the gravelly slope and secured it with a rope tied around a log.

"People camp here, Lex. There's a pit toilet up there," he said, pointing above the beach. "And if you're up for a hike, there's an easy trail to Sea-Bird Point," he added, gesturing east. "From there, we can go up Pandora Hill."

Alexa caught the twinkle in his eye when he mentioned Pandora Hill, though she wasn't sure what sparked it.

After lunch—and a stop at the pit toilet—they followed the trail to Sea-Bird Point, where they paused to watch a small colony of sea lions at the eastern edge of Discovery. From there, they continued up Pandora Hill. Sweeping views of the Olympic Mountains unfolded before them, but it was the abundance of colorful wildflowers in the forest and meadows that took Alexa's breath away.

After taking the ferry from Sunrise to Victoria, they launched from Oak Bay Marina—a shorter route but known for stronger currents. The early morning crossing was peaceful, with calm water, a friendly sky, and a light wind. Dressed in matching red flotation jackets, they paddled together in the double kayak, Alexa seated behind Kevin, enjoying the journey while remaining alert for any changes.

Spotting an opening in the breakwater, they paddled ahead, vigilant for other boaters. The Chain Islands appeared in the distance, with Harris Island providing a suitable spot to assess conditions and check boat traffic in the channel before setting off toward Great Chain Island.

The water was rough, causing Alexa to question her ability to navigate such strong currents.

"Could be a little rough crossing Mayor Channel," Kevin warned. "We might have to ferry glide." After checking the speed and direction of the current, they adjusted the kayak's angle accordingly and aimed for Great Chain Island.

Navigating through the Great Chain Islets, an ecological reserve, they observed harbor seals sunning on exposed rocks, a colony of sea lions, and black oystercatchers—their shrill cries and bright orange beaks making them easy to spot.

They drifted ashore along a stony beach for a short break, straddling driftwood logs and soaking up the rugged beauty of Discovery before continuing.

As currents swirled, they chose a route through the islets leading to Discovery Island. After checking the winds in Plumper Passage, Kevin determined it was safe to cross.

"'We'll ferry glide across the channel, Lexi," he said, angling the kayak slightly. "By paddling at an angle to the current instead of fighting it head-on, we can stay in control and hold our position."

They reached slower waters and eddies near the shoreline where a cluster of driftwood logs had gathered. Kevin guided them in, and they straddled one to stretch their legs and reset before pushing off again.

"We'll head south along the shore and around Commodore Point," Kevin shouted, "to Rudlin Bay. We can land there and have lunch."

"Yay," Alexa cheered, feeling her stomach rumble. "It's time for a break."

The coarse sand and pebbled beach at Rudlin Bay, sheltered from the waves, offered a perfect place to land. Kevin pulled their kayak onto the gravelly slope, securing it with a rope tied around a log on the shore. "People camp here, Lex. There's a pit toilet up there," he said, pointing above the beach. "And if you're up for hiking, there's an easy trail to Sea-Bird Point," he added, pointing east. "From there, we can hike up Pandora Hill."

Alexa noticed a twinkle in Kevin's eye when he mentioned Pandora Hill, though she wasn't sure why.

After lunch and using the pit toilet, they took the trail to Sea-Bird Point, where they admired a small colony of sea lions on the east side of Discovery Island. Upon reaching Pandora Hill, sweeping views of the Olympic Mountains greeted them, but it was the abundance of colourful wildflowers in the forest and meadows that took Alexa's breath away.

"Thank you, Mr. Adventurer," Alexa said, gazing up at Kevin, ruggedly attractive after the paddle. "But I think the winds are a-changin'. Shouldn't we head back?"

"Don't worry, Lex; I'm on top of it," he said confidently. "You're right, both the wind and the currents have shifted. Just follow my lead, okay?"

She had no choice, she thought, settling into her seat behind Kevin.

Sensing it was time to leave the park, they paddled east, back into the channel between Discovery and Chatham Islands. At low tide, the shallow waters revealed sea life beneath the kayak. Crabs, sea urchins, and sea stars delighted them, and a harlequin duck bobbing in the water brought smiles to their faces. As Alexa viewed majestic Mt. Baker in the distance, its snowcapped peak stark white against the blue sky, she murmured, "I love where we live."

Although they had planned to return through the channel between Discovery and Chatham and cross Plumper Passage back to the Chain Islets, working their way to the marina, Kevin reconsidered. The temptation to take the straight line back to the marina outweighed the safer path, but he had experience going this way, and by now, Alexa trusted his guidance.

But things went wrong. With increased exposure to the main channel, the currents intensified. As they struggled to paddle through rough water, the wind shifted against the current. A steep, breaking wave struck their kayak, capsizing it and tossing them into the frigid water.

Desperately trying to climb back into the kayak, Alexa felt like she was attempting to mount a slippery cork. The boat flipped over on top of them twice, each time plunging them back into the sea. Clinging to the side of the kayak with one hand, Kevin rummaged through the storage compartment with the other, eventually retrieving the signal flares. He ignited them, their bright light piercing the overcast sky, then secured both Alexa and himself to the boat, hoping for a swift rescue.

"They'll find us, Alexa," Kevin assured her, his voice steady despite the cold seeping into their bones. "Just stay positive. Picture the heat of a roaring fire."

After what felt like an eternity, the Oak Bay Search and Rescue team arrived within half an hour. Relief washed over Alexa, her eyes filling with tears. Once she was safely out of the water, wrapped in a thermal blanket, sobs overtook her as she contemplated the peril they had narrowly escaped.

THE NEXT TIME Kevin suggested an adventure, Alexa responded with a hint of sarcasm. "How about a hike? Somewhere I can keep my feet on the ground and not risk hypothermia."

"You can get hypothermia anywhere," Kevin replied,

missing her point entirely. "How about paddleboarding on the lake? That way, you can keep your feet on the board," he teased.

Agreeing to hike a section of the East Sooke Trail, a five-and-a-half-hour hike once on Vancouver Island, they'd read about slippery rocks and made sure to wear their grippiest hiking boots.

"Do you mind driving, Lex?" Kevin asked. "We can leave your car at Pike Point, where the trail ends, and then take my truck to the Aylard Farm trailhead to start our hike."

"Good thinking, Kev," Alexa replied. "I haven't gotten my 'hiking legs' yet this year, and five or six hours is a long time."

"Don't worry, sweetie," he reassured her. "We can stop for a lunch break along the way."

The trail lived up to its reputation with lots of rocks and exposed roots, making travel uneven. Combined with the distance and elevation changes and occasional scrambles over rocky sections, Alexa found it challenging. But she tried not to show it.

"We're lucky it's fairly dry," Alexa noted. "I can't imagine trekking through here when it's muddy."

As they reached a vantage point offering sweeping ocean views, Alexa paused, taking it all in.

"The scenery here is breathtaking," she remarked.

"Look," Kevin said, pointing to a colony of sea lions basking on the rocks below. "Reminds me of Discovery..." He trailed off, realizing it was a sensitive topic.

"Nope," she responded firmly. "Not even close."

As Alexa and Kevin continued their hike along the East Sooke Trail, they entered a dense, forested section where sunlight filtered through the canopy, casting dappled shadows on the path. The air was cool and filled with the earthy scent of moss and damp leaves.

Kevin looked down to see a large black slug inching its way

across the trail. He crouched beside it, observing its elongated body and the ridge-like texture along its back.

"That's an Arion rufus, commonly known as the black slug," Kevin said. "They're quite common around here."

"What? Have you studied slugs? Is there anything you don't know, Kev?" Alexa teased.

"There are a few things, but I came across a fascinating children's book in our waiting room called Slimy Slick: The Nighttime Adventures of a Banana Slug."

"It's quite informative about these little creatures and their role in the ecosystem."

Alexa smiled, her curiosity piqued.

"Slugs are fascinating creatures. For instance, did you know that banana slugs are vital to our ecosystem? They act as decomposers, breaking down dead organic matter like fallen leaves and animal droppings, recycling nutrients back into the soil."

Alexa raised an eyebrow. "Really? Who knew?"

"Yep," Kevin continued. "Their slime is also quite remarkable. It acts as both a lubricant and an adhesive, helping them glide over rough terrain or stick to surfaces as needed."

Alexa laughed. "Okay, I stand corrected. Apologies, Mr. Slug or Mrs. Slug, or whoever you are."

Kevin joined in her laughter. "You might not know that some slugs are hermaphroditic, meaning they have both male and female reproductive organs."

Alexa's eyes widened, her focus sharpening as she listened.

"But I'll leave it to you to explore the intriguing world of slug reproduction. He glanced at his watch. "We should keep moving if we want to get back before dark."

As they resumed their hike, Alexa couldn't help but feel a growing appreciation for the unexpected wonders of nature—and for Kevin's enthusiasm in sharing them with her.

After a couple of hours on the trail, fatigue set in.

When Alexa's left knee buckled upon landing on a hard rock, causing her to lose balance, Kevin quickly reached out to steady her.

"Whoa there, babe," he said, concerned. "Maybe it's time to stop for a snack and rest for a bit."

They found a spot on a flat, rocky ledge bathed in sunlight. After half an hour, rehydrated and refreshed, they resumed the trek. "Careful not to trip on the roots, hon," Kevin cautioned her.

Alexa noticed Kevin's attentiveness. She couldn't help but feel that their shared adventures were bringing them closer together.

~

JULY 6, 2024

On the morning of her wedding, Emily awoke to the soft light filtering through her bedroom curtains. Nick had spent the night at Kevin's place, honoring the tradition of not seeing the bride before the ceremony. Her mother, Charlotte, still occupied the guest room down the hall, awaiting the completion of her new home on Stewart's property.

Emily lingered in bed, savoring the significance of the day. As she envisioned the forthcoming events, excitement bubbled within her, making it impossible to remain in bed any longer. Throwing back the duvet, she slipped out of bed, her bare feet padding across the wooden floor to the hexagonal window. Peering outside, she spotted the event coordinator bustling about the grounds, clipboard in hand. A thrill ran through her as she took in the scene—it felt like a dream, like she was a princess in her castle, with the entire day revolving around her and Nick. Eager to savor one final luxurious bubble bath before walking down the aisle, she made her way to the bathroom, anticipation building with every step.

As she soaked in the warm, lavender-scented water, Emily reflected on the journey that had led her to this moment. The challenges and triumphs, the laughter and tears—all had culminated in this day of celebration and love. She felt a deep sense of gratitude for her family and friends, whose efforts had helped transform her life and that of her mother.

After her bath, Emily dried off, wrapped herself in a plush robe, and exited the bathroom. Her elegant wedding gown, a symbol of the commitment she was about to make, hung gracefully on a swing-arm wall hanger, carefully mounted to showcase the dress. Charlotte had lovingly prepared a tray of breakfast items—fresh fruit, a scrambled egg croissant, and a pot of coffee—to ensure Emily remained nourished and energized for her big day.

AMID THE WEDDING PREPARATIONS, Alexa, craving a brief escape from the chaos, decided to take a short walk before changing into her bridesmaid's dress. She wandered toward the newly installed gazebo, delivered in June, seeking a moment of solitude.

Nearby, she noticed a section of ground that appeared slightly sunken, perhaps unsettled, from recent construction. Intrigued, she stepped closer to investigate.

Dense vegetation tangled the area. Using her foot, she swept aside some of the overgrowth, uncovering several weathered wooden planks and rotting boards. As she pulled away more debris, an opening emerged. Alexa crouched for a closer look.

Without warning, the fragile edge crumbled beneath her weight, collapsing into a dark abyss. She plummeted into the void, the fall swift and unforgiving. Her flailing arms scraped against the rough stone walls before her head struck hard, the impact plunging her into unconsciousness. Twelve feet below, she landed in a layer of wet mud, her body twisted awkwardly in the cold, damp isolation of the forgotten shaft. Amid the wedding day's hustle and bustle, Alexa's absence went unnoticed, leaving her stranded and unconscious, with little chance of discovery before it was too late.

The well, an ancient relic from the island's earliest settlers, faded from memory over generations. Crudely constructed by digging deep into the soil to access the water table and lining the walls with rough-hewn fieldstones, its structure remained intact despite long abandonment. A parched summer had left the well dry, sparing Alexa from the threat of drowning—but offering no solace in the cold, suffocating silence that enveloped her.

BACK AT THE HOUSE, Rollo's restlessness grew. The loyal dog sensed something was amiss and began circling the area near the gazebo, whining and pawing at the disturbed ground. His behavior drew the attention of a few guests, but with the wedding imminent, most were too preoccupied to look into it further.

As Emily nibbled on a strawberry, there was a soft knock at the door. "Come in," she called, her voice bubbling with excitement.

The door opened, and Kyla bounced in, with Charlotte close behind her.

"Good morning, beautiful bride," Kyla greeted, enveloping Emily in a warm hug.

"Morning," Emily replied, smiling affectionately at her soon-to-be sister-in-law. "I can't believe the day is finally here."

"Believe it," Charlotte interjected with a grin. "Now, let's get you ready to marry the love of your life."

The room buzzed with joyful energy as the hairstylist and makeup artist arrived, setting up their stations. Emily glanced at her mother, Charlotte's eyes misty with emotion as she watched her daughter transform into a bride. The photographer snapped candid moments—the laughter, the shared stories, and even Kyla taking a big bite of an hors d'oeuvre— perfectly capturing the vibe of the morning.

"Where's Alexa?" Emily asked Kyla.

"I was wondering the same thing, Em. It's not like her to be late."

Emily's heart raced with a blend of excitement and concern. She tried to steady herself, though Alexa's absence lingered in her mind. "And Lexi's missing all the fun."

"I'll go ask Mom," Kyla replied, hurrying away. "She usually knows what's happening," she said over her shoulder as she exited the room.

With the final touches applied, Emily stood before the full-length mirror, taking in her reflection. The gown fit her perfectly, its intricate lace and flowing fabric embodying both elegance and grace. Her hair, styled in soft waves and adorned with delicate flowers that complemented her bouquet, framed her face perfectly. The makeup enhanced her natural beauty, a radiant glow shining from within.

"You look stunning," Charlotte whispered, her voice thick with emotion.

"Thank you, Mom," Emily replied, tears welling in her eyes. "I couldn't have done any of this without you."

A gentle knock interrupted the moment. "It's time," the event coordinator announced softly.

Emily took a deep breath, her heart racing with nervous excitement. Even though Kyla still had not returned to the room, she assumed the twins were downstairs, where they'd join the rest of the bridal party.

As Emily descended the staircase, her gown flowing gracefully, she couldn't shake the nagging worry about Alexa. Glancing across the living room, Emily's eyes searched for her. Instead, they landed on Izzy, adorable in a pink tulle dress with a matching headband, nestled among rose petals in the wagon Jude would pull down the grassy aisle.

Emily turned to Charlotte, her eyes revealing deep concern. "I don't see Alexa, Mom. Where is she?"

As the ceremony's start time approached and Alexa's absence had become more conspicuous, concern intensified. Jennie's initial irritation turned to panic. Alarm rippled through the guests as a small search party looked for Alexa.

"Kyla," Charlotte called, "Have you seen Alexa? Does your mom know where she is?"

Kyla approached, her brow furrowed. "We don't know where she is, even Kevin. I'm so sorry, Emily. I've phoned, texted, asked everyone who might know something...."

Tension escalated as the bridal party assembled, unaware of Alexa's predicament. Minutes felt like hours, and the joyous atmosphere waned as concern for Alexa's whereabouts and well-being grew.

Charlotte's worried eyes locked on those of Sarah, the event coordinator. "What now?" she asked, bewildered.

"The show must go on," Sarah said confidently. Then, turning to Emily, she said, "These things happen. Please don't let it spoil your special day. Sometimes people are late, that's all. When Alexa arrives, we'll simply fit her in as if nothing happened."

As Emily stepped into the late afternoon sunlight, the assembled guests turned to behold the bride, their faces lighting up with admiration and joy. Emily's gaze locked onto Nick's, and in that instant, all the planning, all the waiting, culminated in a single, breathtaking moment of connection.

The wedding ceremony unfolded with heartfelt vows, exchanged rings, and the sealing kiss that marked the beginning of their married life. Surrounded by the beauty of nature and the warmth of their community, Emily and Nick's love story entered a new chapter, one that promised a lifetime of shared dreams and unwavering partnership.

As Nick and Emily walked back down the aisle, attendees stood, applauding, some throwing confetti as they strolled arm-in-arm, beaming with joy. It was Rollo's persistent barking near the gazebo that eventually drew Clay's attention. The dog's restlessness grew as he circled the gazebo, whining and pawing at the disturbed ground.

Hurrying over to investigate, Clay and Patrick stopped short when they noticed the opening in the ground. A sick feeling rose in Clay's stomach. "Patrick," he said, trying to remain calm. "Run over to the barn and grab the flashlights... quick!"

Patrick raced to the barn and back, drawing the attention of some guests Clay peered into the darkness, his stomach churning as he spotted Alexa's motionless form at the bottom.

"Patrick, call 911—it's urgent," he said, his voice tight with fear.

Clay's mind frantically searched for a way to get Alexa safely out of the well. Seeing the commotion, Jude raced over, assessed the situation, and flew to the barn, returning with a long, thick rope, a roll of twine, and a hammock from the storage shed.

Other wedding guests joined them at the site, forming a human chain to help lower Jude into the well safely. Once he reached Alexa, his fingers detected a weak pulse, and he knew they had to get her out fast. "Feed a second rope down here," he shouted to the others. "I'll wrap her in the hammock and tie it to the two ropes, and you can pull her up that way."

Cocooning Alexa's body into the hammock and securing the ends with twine, he bound it to the two ropes. "Okay, we're ready," he shouted. "Pull her up slowly."

By the time Alexa's body reached the surface, everyone had

gathered, tears in their eyes as she regained consciousness, disoriented but alive, her head smeared with mud. The realization of how close they came to losing her cast a somber shadow over the wedding celebration.

Jennie rushed to her daughter's side. "Lexi, honey, you're going to be okay," she managed, trying to believe her own words. Kevin helped free Alexa from the wrappings, then stepped aside to let the ambulance attendants do their work.

Jennie and Kyla rode in the ambulance while Kevin, Clay, and Patrick followed behind. Jennie had convinced Nick and Emily to carry on with the celebration, promising to report any updates as they came. Bev stepped in to comfort Kathleen while they awaited more news.

"No broken bones," Bev reported to Kathleen as soon as Jennie called. "She has a concussion, and they'll keep her overnight to monitor it, but they think she'll be fine."

Kathleen's eyes filled with tears of joy. "It's a miracle she's alive," she said, her voice trembling. "And on today, of all days."

Bev wrapped her arms around Kathleen, holding her until she calmed. "It IS a miracle, Kathleen. Now, why don't you sit here by the fire and I'll make you a cup of warm milk, just in case the sandman forgot you needed to get some sleep tonight?"

Kathleen smiled warmly, wiping a tear from her cheek. "Would you mind asking Nick and Emily to step in and see me before I turn in for the night?" she asked.

"SHE'S GOING TO BE OKAY," Nick announced, taking the mic from the lead singer of their favourite local band. Cheers and applause erupted through the crowd. "Here's to Alexa," he continued, raising his glass.

Relief washed over the celebration, softening the earlier

shock into something more fragile—gratitude, still edged with disbelief.

The celebration continued with a heightened sense of gratitude, the family holding each other a little closer that night. Laughter punctuated the gathering once more as guests entertained themselves at the photo booth and wandered among the food stalls, the ice-cream cart, and the open bar.

Nick and Emily would cherish their wedding for years to come, and Alexa's story would be told again and again. For now, though, it was simply the start of something new—a marriage, a testament to the love they had nurtured and the future they would build together.

4

ROLLO

From the corner of her eye, Jennie noticed a flash of red —Clay's winter jacket standing out against the muted tones of the barn. As he slowly approached the verandah, his head bowed, she could tell something was wrong. A choked sob escaped him. 'I'm so sorry,' he said, stepping onto the wooden floor. "It's Rollo." With tears in his eyes, he glanced at Kyla, knowing she and Alexa had loved their loyal German pointer all their lives.

"Is he... gone?" Kyla asked, her voice barely a whisper.

"I'm afraid so," Clay replied. "Found him in Music's stall, lying in the soft hay."

Kyla and Jennie hurried toward the barn, with Clay not far behind. Their sadness hung heavily in the air as Kyla and Jennie crouched beside Rollo, tears streaming down Kyla's face. She reached out and gently stroked his head, the stillness of the barn wrapping around her.

Jennie broke the silence, speaking in a hushed tone. "He was fourteen, dear. That's pretty incredible."

"And he lived a dog's best life here at the farm," Clay added. "Not that it makes it any easier, Kye, I don't mean that."

"I know, Clay. It's just a shock. We all knew his time was coming ..." Kyla said, her voice trailing off.

"And to think his last heroic act was saving Alexa's life," Jennie said, her voice catching with the effort to hold back tears. The words broke them all, and Jennie stood, pacing slowly to steady herself.

"If you want to spend more time with him, Kye, I'll let the others know," Clay said, reaching for a nearby horse blanket. "You can cover him with this, and when everyone's ready, I'll bury him in the apple orchard."

"Thanks, Clay," Jennie said, her smile soft as she looked up at him. "I'm glad you're here to handle this. I'm sure we'll all want to be there when you lay him to rest."

The silence between them was heavy with memories—Rollo's loyalty, his calming presence, and the many ways he had touched their lives. Kyla and Jennie stayed kneeling beside him, the reality of their loss settling around them.

Finally, Kyla wiped her eyes and stood, brushing stray bits of straw from her knees. "Let's go tell the others," she whispered. Jennie nodded, reaching out to give her arm a quick, reassuring squeeze.

LATER, as they gathered in the living room, the house felt quieter and emptier. The space, once filled with Rollo's joyful presence, now seemed to echo with his absence. Jennie sat down beside Kyla, who looked up at her with red-rimmed eyes. "It's hard to believe he's gone," Kyla said softly. "It's like a part of the farm is missing."

Jennie didn't answer right away. Instead, she reached over and squeezed Kyla's hand, unable to find words for it. The heaviness of the day lingered, settling over them in the quiet of the room.

5

———

CHARLOTTE

The briny scent of the Salish Sea enveloped Charlotte and Emily as they strolled around the harbour, gazing at the sailboats lining the dock. They were meeting for lunch at the Sandpiper Seafood Bar and Grill, a new waterfront restaurant that had quickly become the talk of the town.

"Let's sit outside, shall we?" Emily gestured toward a vacant table, the sea breeze tousling her hair.

"Yes, as long as we can get a table with an umbrella," her mother replied.

They settled in with a view of the harbour and the sun shining overhead. After scanning the menu, Charlotte ordered the clam chowder with homemade focaccia while Emily ordered freshly shucked oysters, their house specialty.

"Here we are," Charlotte said, glancing out at the view. "When I compare my new life to what I left behind, Em..." Her voice trailed off, her eyes lingering on the horizon.

"Mom, I can't tell you how happy I feel now that you've moved here. To have lunch with you like this, to have you here to visit whenever I want..." Emily's voice wavered as her thoughts drifted to how things might have been. She reached for her water glass, the cold against her fingers grounding her.

Touched, Charlotte's expression softened. "I feel the same way, Em. This is more than I ever dreamed of."

They exchanged a smile, the kind that spoke volumes without needing words. "I'm excited to see my new home... well, you know what I mean... the home Stewart had Patrick build for me," Charlotte added.

"I can't wait to see it, Mom.

"Let's stop at the bakery stand on the way to Stewart's place and grab him a loaf of that dill bread. It's one of his favorites."

"Or maybe he'd prefer some cider," Charlotte suggested.

"Or," Emily replied with a smile, "we could save that for ourselves. I'm guessing Stewart's tastes are pretty simple, Mom. I don't think the cidery offerings would mean much to him."

Charlotte chuckled softly. "We wouldn't want to waste that on him, then. But when I get my first paycheck, maybe I can treat you and Nick to a dinner out."

Emily wasn't sure how quickly her mother expected things to settle, but she suspected Charlotte would want to get her financial bearings before treating anyone to dinner. "That's sweet, Mom. No rush. We'll go there together sometime."

THE ISLANDS TRUST Land Use Bylaw permitted the construction of an accessory dwelling on Stewart's fifty-acre property. Thanks to community volunteers working under Stewart's direction, it was completed in under a year—a remarkable feat during a construction boom when both labor and materials were in short supply. Securing the right supplies and arranging their delivery to the island was a challenge of its own.

From the front gate, Charlotte peered at the new home, its

light-coloured exterior visible in the distance. It stood fifty feet away from the main house. "We're going to plant a laurel hedge, maybe a row of poplars, for more privacy," she said to Emily, whose delight was unmistakable.

"Evergreen—that's the key," Emily replied.

"I know," Charlotte said with a smile, "but who can resist a row of poplars?

Stewart was already at the front door when they pulled into the driveway of the new house, dressed in his standard tweed jacket and baggy trousers.

"Afternoon, ladies," he greeted with a tip of his hat. "What do you think so far, Charlotte?"

"Oh, please, call me Lottie; everyone does. Makes me feel like back home."

"Okay, Lottie," Stewart replied, "What's your first impression of Warren Manor?" he teased, waiting for her reaction.

"Can this really be my new home?" Charlotte asked. "I mean, of course, it isn't my home," she clarified, feeling awkward. "You know what I mean..."

"Well," Stewart said, swinging open the front door. "It'll take some work to make it a home, I'm sure."

Charlotte gasped when the open-plan kitchen, living room, and dining room came into view, sunlight streaming through the expansive windows. "Oh, it's much bigger than it looks outside. It's beautiful, Stewart; I love it."

But even as she spoke, her mind betrayed her, pulling her back to the crumbling home she'd once shared with her husband. She could almost hear the sharp crack of glass shattering against the kitchen floor, feel the suffocating weight of anticipation, her heart lodged in her throat as she braced for the sound of his footsteps returning. The fear lingered, clinging to her like a shadow she couldn't escape.

She couldn't help herself. She stepped toward Stewart and wrapped her arms around him, holding tight, seeking an anchor in the calm he exuded. But when he didn't hug back, her confidence wavered. Releasing him quickly, she stepped back, her cheeks heating.

Her heart sank like a stone. Did I overstep?

"I should have asked before hugging you. I'm sorry," she murmured, glancing at the floor.

"Oh no, don't worry. It's me, not you," Stewart replied gently. "It's been twenty-seven years since I lost Amelia, so... I guess I've become a bit of a stranger to hugs."

"I'm so sorry, Stewart," Charlotte said, her voice soft. "Do you have family nearby?"

"Other than the Mitchells, you mean?" he replied with a grin. "Amelia and I had two children—grown now and living off the island. And I have two grandboys, ages eighteen and twenty-one. They spent a lot of time with me here on the farm."

"I'm sure they loved it here, Stewart," Emily chimed in. "Kids seem to gravitate toward the natural life, don't you think?"

"The lucky ones who get exposed to it," Stewart said. "Sometimes people who grow up in the city think country folk are backward, but I've learned it's often just inexperience talking."

The faint scent of fresh paint lingered in the air, mingling with the distant hum of honeybees drifting through the open window.

"Mom," Emily said suddenly, her voice brimming with excitement, "get a load of that fireplace."

Between the living and dining areas stood a see-through gas fireplace, its solid oak mantel nestled in a fieldstone wall.

"I'm in heaven, Em," she said. Then, turning to Stewart, "I can't thank you enough. This is far beyond my expectations...I didn't really have expectations... I just wanted a job and a place to live."

Stewart hesitated at the door, his hand lingering on the

knob. "Take your time," he said, his voice softer now. Then he stepped outside, the door clicking shut behind him.

～

AT 8:00 A.M. SHARP, Charlotte knocked on Stewart's front door, her knuckles brushing against a rusted knocker where the name Owen was barely visible through years of wear. When the door opened, Stewart stood before her, his usual rugged attire replaced with lighter clothes better suited to the July heat. Without his cap, the deep lines on his face and his thinning hair were more noticeable. He offered her a faint smile, but his eyes carried a seriousness that made Charlotte's chest tighten. Was it suspicion—or something else—lingering there?

"I'll give you the grand tour," he said with a grin, "and then leave you to figure out the rest."

Starting with the kitchen, he pointed to an old wood stove. "That was my grandmother's. We'd stick a long-handled fork into a slice of her thick, homemade bread and toast it over the flame." He chuckled, the memory lighting his face. "With a slather of homemade butter? You've never had toast like that—I guarantee it," he added proudly.

The living room was sparse. An old stuffed chair sat beside a floor lamp that looked like it might release clouds of dust if she touched it. The matching sofa and cushions were as drab and weary as Stewart's standard attire—probably just as dirty, Charlotte guessed. She scanned the room, looking for open windows, but they were closed, curtains drawn tight, blinds drawn tight.

"There's one room you don't have to worry about cleaning," Stewart said as they walked down a short hallway toward the stairs. He stopped in front of a door, tapped it for emphasis, and said, "I keep it locked all the time. Don't need it anymore. Saves on heat."

"Okay," Charlotte replied. "Noted."

After a quick tour of the upstairs, Charlotte returned downstairs to assess the cleaning supplies. In a closet, she found a plastic pail, some rags, a box of Borax, and a misshapen broom with a dustpan. The Electrolux vacuum cleaner looked promising, and there was even a box of extra filters. Under the kitchen sink, she found a box of dishwasher soap, liquid dish detergent, a scrub brush, and a box of garbage bags.

She loaded the breakfast dishes into the dishwasher and cleaned the sink, countertops, and small appliances. Opening the kitchen blinds, she noted that both the blinds and the windows needed cleaning—but that would be a task for another day. Time slipped by, and at 4:00, Charlotte put away the cleaning tools and stepped out the front door.

In the yard, Stewart stood by his pickup truck, the hood open. She walked over to join him.

"Stewart, I'm done for the day," she said with a smile. "I'll go at it hard the first few days to give everything a thorough cleaning. After that, I doubt you'll need me from 8:00 to 4:00 every day."

Stewart straightened up from the truck and listened as she spoke. "Okay, that sounds good. We'll adjust as we go, depending... well, on how things unfold, I guess."

"Agreed," Charlotte said. "This is all new to me, too. But let me know if there's anything you don't like or if I've missed something."

"Yep," he replied with a nod. "You have a good night now. See you tomorrow."

Charlotte headed toward her house, the warm summer evening wrapping around her like a gift. She still couldn't quite believe that the home up ahead was hers—at least for now.

～

AFTER THE FIRST WEEK, they settled into a routine. Charlotte would buy groceries every Monday, planning meals for the week. Wednesday became laundry day. Dinner was on the table by 6:00, Monday through Thursday. Mondays were for cleaning downstairs, and Fridays for upstairs. Weather permitting, she'd tend the garden as needed, depending on the season.

Things went smoothly until she offered to take Stewart's tweed jacket and baggy brown pants to the dry cleaner. She even risked suggesting his hat could use a cleaning.

"Dry cleaning?" he grimaced. "I can't stand the smell of dry cleaning. That's why I hang these duds on the clothesline—give them a good airing out now and then."

"Yes," Charlotte said, nodding. "Air-dried clothes smell great, I agree. But, Stewart, there's a lot of dirt on these clothes that won't come off with a brush. And by the way, we have wet cleaners in town now. None of that smell you're talking about."

Stewart's face twisted into a pained expression. "That so? They're wool, you know. The cleaners might ruin them. It's my favorite outfit."

"I know," Charlotte replied, stifling a laugh. "Tell you what —I'll ask them specifically about cleaning wool. If they can't guarantee it, I won't leave them there. Sound good?"

Stewart stood still for a moment, weighing the offer. "Okay, good enough, Charlotte. I'll gather them up for you."

"Great. Let's put them in this large garbage bag to keep the car clean, okay?"

A few minutes later, Stewart returned, the garbage bag bulging with his clothes. He handed it to her solemnly, as if entrusting her with a great responsibility. "Good luck," he said gravely.

~

CHARLOTTE GREW accustomed to the rhythm of Stewart's farm —the creak of the barn doors in the morning, the scent of hay mingling with the sweet fragrance of ripened fruit, and Stewart's gruff but steady presence. But today there was an unusual stillness in the house.

"Stewart?" Charlotte called, balancing the crate of eggs she'd brought in from the coop.

"In here," his voice came faintly from somewhere down the hall.

Charlotte set the crate on the kitchen counter and followed the sound. The short hallway leading to the stairs was dim, lit only by the afternoon sunlight spilling in from the sitting room opposite.

As she passed the closed door on the left, something about it held her attention—maybe the polished wood, out of place against the house's rustic charm. Or perhaps it was Stewart's earlier words: "Don't need it anymore. Saves on heat."

She caught herself lingering, feeling foolish for letting a door hold her curiosity. She shook her head and walked toward the study at the end of the hall.

"Stewart?" she called again, stepping inside to find him sitting at the desk, a scattering of receipts and notebooks in front of him.

"Didn't mean to interrupt," she said softly, noting the slight frown on his face as he gathered the papers into a neat stack.

"You're not interrupting," he said, rising and slipping the papers into a drawer. "Just going over some numbers. Always something to do around here."

"I'm curious," Charlotte said. "Do you ever go into that room... or does the door stay shut all the time?"

Stewart looked at her sharply, then softened, letting out a heavy sigh.

"Some doors are best left closed," he said finally, his voice heavy. Then he pushed back his chair and brushed past her on his way out of the study.

Charlotte stayed behind, her curiosity sharpened rather than satisfied. It wasn't like Stewart to sidestep a question. As her eyes drifted to the desk, she noticed a single photograph lying face down. Turning it over, she saw a younger Stewart, arm-in-arm with a woman who must have been Amelia, her smile radiant.

When she caught up with him in the kitchen, he was rinsing a coffee mug.

"Everything alright?" she asked, watching his face.

"Fine," he said, though his voice had a slight edge. "Plenty to keep me busy."

Charlotte nodded but couldn't shake the feeling that Stewart's answer had little to do with the chores on the farm—and everything to do with what lay behind that locked door.

In the middle of her second week working at Stewart's place, Charlotte's phone chimed with a call from her sister Lizzy in England.

"He's dead, Lottie," Lizzy said, her voice sharp and direct as if Charlotte should immediately know who she meant. "Struck by a transport truck trying to cross the road—higher than a kite, they said. Killed instantly."

Charlotte froze, her breath catching at the sudden news of her husband Fred's death. For a moment, she couldn't find the words. "How... how did you find out, Liz?"

"When the police couldn't reach you, they called me. I said I'd contact you and Em."

Charlotte sank into a chair, her thoughts swirling. She told no one where she'd gone when she fled England—not even her closest friends. All Lizzy had was a phone number. Charlotte wanted to make sure Fred couldn't find her, no matter how hard he tried. She thought she should feel sad that Fred was gone, but a quiet relief settled over her.

Emily was treating a patient when Charlotte called the clinic. Their receptionist, Ginny, said she'd give Dr. Emily the message to call her mother as soon as she was free.

As she crossed the waiting room, Emily asked her next patient to settle into Treatment Room Two, and she'd be in shortly. The news of her father's death hit Emily like a wave, leaving her numb.

"Is something wrong, Dr. Emily?" Ginny asked, noticing the paleness of her face and how she'd grown quiet.

"It's okay, Ginny," she said. "Everything's okay." Emily returned to her treatment room in a fog. Fortunately, her patient was a regular with no new symptoms, and all went smoothly.

At lunchtime, Emily drove to see her mother at Stewart's farm. They hugged each other for a long time, in silence, and Stewart left the room, giving them privacy. When he returned, asking, "Is everything alright?", Charlotte replied, "My husband Fred died, and we'll have to return to England and arrange his funeral, Stewart. Do you mind if I take a few days off to take care of it?"

"Not at all," Stewart replied, his voice uncertain. "I'm sorry for your... loss."

Yes, Stewart. At this stage, it's all about the logistics," she said, her voice steady despite the tears glistening in her eyes. "But I mourn the man I fell in love with before his addiction," she continued. "Those are the memories I'll hold onto as we lay him to rest."

~

CHARLOTTE AND EMILY returned from England. Another chapter closed as surely as the coffin lay in the ground.

"Em, I feel lighter now. Coming back to Sunrise Island unencumbered makes me feel energized somehow."

"I know what you mean, Mum. Even for me, it feels like the start of a new life."

On her first day back at work, Charlotte noticed Stewart was not his usual spirited self. She didn't want to pry, but her concern deepened when he didn't show up for dinner that evening.

The next morning, as she arrived to start her chores, Stewart greeted her with a wistful expression. "Amelia used to make the best damson plum jam," he said. "Nothing like it."

"We had a plum tree in our yard back home, Stewart. If you like, I can put up a few jars for you."

"These are damson plums, you know," he said, lowering his chin and peering up at her.

"I know exactly what you're talking about," Charlotte replied with a laugh, "Trust me, I know how special the damsons are."

"I'll get my grandson Noah to harvest the plums. He's coming tomorrow—just popping in on his way to Saturna. Going camping with his buddies."

"Do you always put your grandsons to work when they visit?" Charlotte teased.

"Oh, those boys know all about farmwork—that's why they're chasing careers in technology instead," Stewart said, his eyes brightening.

"Smart boys," Charlotte quipped. "If Noah picks the plums tomorrow morning, I'll start the process in the afternoon... assuming you've got all the supplies we'll need."

"Amelia had everything we needed," he said, his voice softening, eyes downcast.

~

THE NEXT MORNING, Charlotte filled a spray bottle with vinegar, ready to wash the windows before the afternoon sun made streak-free drying a challenge.

How long has it been since these were cleaned? She wondered, swiping a finger over the glass and leaving a clear streak. Using a kitchen chair, she climbed onto the countertop to clean the upper windows, then stood carefully on the counter for the highest sections. Outside, she'd already set up a stepladder on the porch to tackle the exterior windows.

With the kitchen and living room windows finished, she took a break on the porch swing. Her gaze drifted down the long gravel laneway toward the roadside stand. Maybe Stewart would let me sell baked goods there, she mused. In the distance, the hum of a tractor reached her ears. Operating machinery was one of the few tasks Stewart could still manage without aggravating his arthritis.

Back inside, Charlotte gathered her cleaning supplies and made her way down the hallway toward the den. As she passed the locked door, an inexplicable heaviness settled over her. She paused, glancing over her shoulder at the door. An irresistible urge to know more crept in as she examined the wreath hanging there—a circle of grapevines adorned with dried eucalyptus, rosehips, herbs, forget-me-nots, pinecones, and acorns.

Reaching out, she touched a cluster of blue forget-me-nots. A flower head broke loose and fell to the floor. Gasping, she watched it fall, its brittle petals scattering like dust. She sneezed and stepped back, realizing the wreath had become a fragile relic, likely shedding pieces with every movement. It must lose pieces every time the door opens—if it even opens, she thought.

On impulse, she tested the handle—and froze. It turned, unlocking with a soft click. Her heart pounded as she hesitated, torn between caution and curiosity. Finally, she edged the door open, holding her breath as she peeked inside.

The room was cold and dim, the air heavy and stale, as if it had been sealed off for decades. At first glance, it seemed almost empty. A dressing table stood against the far wall, its oval mirror clouded with age. The bench beneath it sat undisturbed, as though waiting for someone to return and take a seat.

Framed photographs covered an entire wall, their glass fronts coated in a fine layer of dust. On the end wall, vibrant floral canvases painted in oil brightened the gloom, their rich colors standing out against the room's lifelessness.

Charlotte's gaze drifted to the dressing table where an unfinished painting perched on a stand, brushstrokes frozen mid-creation. Beside it sat a tarnished silver hairbrush, its bristles clinging to clusters of hair, a poignant trace of the woman who'd once owned it.

Near the closet door, a pink sundress hung on its hook, the colour faded in the dim light. Charlotte stepped closer, unable to look away. Dark pink diagonal stripes added a playful sophistication. The fine details—the shirred bodice, the covered buttons running down the front, the wide, flowing skirt—gave it an elegance straight out of a Sophia Loren film. Turning the tag over, she saw it was made in Italy.

Her curiosity deepened. She opened the closet door carefully, half-expecting it to creak, but it swung silently on its hinges. Inside hung half a dozen dresses, their timeless elegance speaking to Amelia's style. On the shelf above, a cream-colored leather purse and matching heels sat neatly together, as if waiting for an outing that would never come.

Closing the door quietly, Charlotte's attention shifted to the chest in the corner. It looked well-worn, its wood scratched and faded. Her pulse quickened. She crouched down and hesitated before lifting the lid.

The lid creaked faintly as she opened it. Inside lay three pieces of jewelry: a heavy gold necklace with a blue topaz pendant bordered by diamonds, an equally weighty gold bracelet, and a wedding ring set. She picked up the rings, turning them over in her fingers.

She placed them back carefully, her palms sweating. As she closed the lid, she told herself she'd leave, but her eyes drifted to the floor near the chest. A faint rectangular outline in the wood caught her attention.

She crouched down again and lifted the lid by the small metal ring attached to it.

Her breath caught as she lifted the lid, revealing a hidden compartment. Inside were several small safes, their surfaces smooth and pristine despite the years. Each was secured with a combination lock. A shiver ran down her spine.

Guilt surged within her. She carefully closed the compartment, her heart pounding. She had already gone too far.

As Charlotte turned toward the door, she froze. A male voice cut through the silence.

"Grandpa's always been strange about that room. Even though we're not allowed in there."

Her heart leaped into her throat. Slowly, she looked up to see a tall young man standing in the doorway. He had to be Noah.

"Oh," she stammered, forcing a smile. "I'm Charlotte. Your grandfather's caregiver and housekeeper." She extended her hand, hoping her voice didn't betray her nerves.

Noah shook her hand with a faint smile. "I figured. Grandpa mentioned you." His eyes darted toward the door.

Charlotte turned and quickly locked it, testing the knob to ensure it was secure. "I was washing windows," she explained, her words tumbling out. "I noticed the door was ajar, so I opened it to lock it again."

Noah frowned slightly but didn't comment. "Grandpa's

getting on in years. He must've forgotten. That's not like him, though."

"There's a first time for everything," she said lightly, praying he wouldn't press the matter. "Can I fix you a sandwich before you head out?"

He chuckled. "No thanks. I've got a ferry to catch. Just came to say goodbye to Grandpa."

"Nice meeting you, Noah," she said, forcing her most casual tone.

"You too, Charlotte." He gave her a quick nod before heading down the hall.

The moment the front door clicked shut behind Noah, Charlotte released a shaky breath she hadn't realized she was holding. Her heart pounded like an unrelenting drum, a constant reminder of their tense encounter. She gathered her window-cleaning supplies, her hands trembling as she forced herself to move. Walking to the den, she tried to focus on her task, but her thoughts kept circling back to the room. The photographs, the dresses, the hidden compartment—why, after twenty-seven years, did Stewart keep this shrine to Amelia? And as much as she tried to shake it off, the burden of her intrusion—and the unsettling question of why Stewart clung so fiercely to the past—clung to her like a shadow.

"You can keep the money from any sales you make on weekends. Since it's weekend work, it won't interfere with the work you do for me."

Stewart readily agreed to let Charlotte sell her homemade goods at his roadside stand. The way he phrased it—"it won't interfere with what you do for me"—caught her off guard. *Maybe he values what I do, after all*, she thought, a quiet sense of appreciation taking hold.

Charlotte adjusted the empty cookie tray in her hands, mentally calculating how many more batches she'd need before the afternoon rush. As she turned toward the house, movement at the edge of her vision caught her eye—a man standing by the stand, watching her.

He wasn't young, but something about him radiated a calm confidence. Faint smile lines crinkled at the corners of his eyes, softening his rugged appearance. Dressed in well-worn jeans and a button-down shirt, he looked as though he belonged on a ranch or behind the wheel of a pickup truck. His gaze lingered —not invasive, but long enough to make her take notice.

She glanced down and quickened her pace. It wasn't the first time she'd drawn a stranger's interest since moving to Sunrise, but something about this man unsettled her. She couldn't pinpoint why.

Don't read into it, she told herself. Men always want something. Always.

By the time she reached her front door, her neck and shoulders were tight, her excitement over cookie sales dulled by an undercurrent of caution.

"WHO WAS that man staring at you from the stand?" Stewart asked, placing a beef roast into the outdoor fridge. Someone had scrawled Jennie Mitchell's name across the brown paper wrapping in bold black marker.

Charlotte adjusted the envelopes of cookies in her basket, lining them up with careful precision. "Oh," she replied lightly. "You noticed him, too."

"How could I not?" Stewart's voice carried a sharper edge than perhaps he intended. "He was ogling you like that."

Charlotte hesitated, her hands pausing mid-motion. "I don't know who he is," she said, a hint of discomfort crossing her face. Then she added with a faint smile, "But... thanks for looking out for me, Stewart."

~

IT WASN'T until the following weekend that Charlotte saw the man again.

Setting her display baskets alongside the rows of fruit and vegetables Stewart had arranged for sale, Charlotte glanced up as the rumble of a pickup truck drew her attention. The vehicle pulled into a spot near the stand, and as the afternoon sun bathed the area in golden light, Charlotte's gaze narrowed. He stepped out of the truck and walked toward her with a confidence that made her feel like she, not the goods, was on display.

"Hi," he said with a grin that was all teeth, the kind that might've been charming if it didn't feel practised. "I couldn't leave without complimenting the baker of those cookies I've been hearing so much about."

Charlotte laughed softly. "Oh, thank you," she replied, keeping her tone polite but cautious. "I hope they live up to the praise."

"I'm sure they will," he said smoothly, his eyes scanning the cookies before settling back on her. "Greg, by the way." He extended his hand, the move a little too calculated, she thought.

"Charlotte," she replied, shaking his hand briefly. His grip was firm, almost overly so, as if he were trying too hard to make an impression. "Are you a regular at the stand—I'm new here."

"Not as much as I'd like to be," Greg said, leaning casually on the table. "But I'm glad I came today. Looks like I picked the right time." He gestured toward the cookies, then to her. "What else do you bake?"

"Oh, a little of everything," Charlotte said, a touch wary of

84

the intensity in his gaze. "Cookies, bread, muffins... nothing too fancy."

"Sounds like you're being modest," he said with a chuckle. "How about this—you tell me your favorite coffee spot in town, and I'll take you there? You can tell me all your baking secrets."

Charlotte hesitated, her instincts kicking in. Something about his demeanor felt too smooth, too practiced. Yet Emily had encouraged her to socialize more, hinting that she might even want to date. His offer was casual enough, and maybe coffee wasn't such a bad idea. "Um, there's the Treehouse Café," she said, glancing at the time on her phone. "It's a nice spot."

"Perfect. How about tomorrow afternoon?" Greg asked, his grin widening. "My treat."

Before Charlotte could answer, Stewart appeared from behind the stand, his presence as solid and grounding as ever. His eyes glanced from Greg to Charlotte, his expression unreadable.

"Everything okay here?" he asked, his tone even but edged with something Charlotte couldn't quite place.

"Just fine," Greg said smoothly, holding out a hand. "Greg. And you are?"

"Stewart," he replied, shaking Greg's hand briefly before turning his attention back to Charlotte. "I'll be around if you need anything."

Charlotte nodded, her cheeks warming. "Thanks, Stewart."

As Stewart walked away, Greg chuckled. "Looks like I've got competition," he said lightly, but there was an edge to his voice that made Charlotte feel uneasy.

THE NEXT DAY, Charlotte sat at a corner table in the Treehouse Café, watching Greg over the rim of her coffee cup. He was charming, but there was something about the way he talked—

too many compliments, too many questions—that left her feeling slightly off-balance.

"So," Greg said, leaning forward, "what do you think? Have I convinced you I'm not so bad after all?"

Charlotte managed a polite smile. "You seem... nice," she said carefully, unsure why she felt the need to hedge her words.

The door jingled as it opened, and Bev breezed in, her fiery red hair impossible to miss. Charlotte's face lit up. Bev had been a pillar of support during some of her darkest days, and seeing her again brought a rush of joy, like catching up with a dear friend after too much time apart.

"Lottie, how lovely to see you—it's been far too long," Bev said, pausing by the table on her way to the counter.

Charlotte smiled warmly, but she couldn't ignore Bev's expression shift from cheerful to guarded as she glanced at Greg.

"Far too long, Bev. We need a proper catch-up. Come by for tea one day?"

"Love to, Bev replied, her cheerfulness tempered. "Let me grab some caffeine, and I'll pop over for a minute, alright?" She moved to the counter, pulling out her phone as she waited in line.

Greg leaned back in his chair, his grin faltering ever so slightly. "I'll use the facilities and grab us refills," he said, standing. "Black, right?"

Charlotte nodded, her unease growing as she watched him walk away Bev, now free from his earshot, slid into the seat across from her, her tone warm but urgent. "Lottie," she said, leaning closer, "do you mind if I steal a second?"

Of course," Charlotte said, although her heart sank at the seriousness in Bev's expression.

Bev glanced toward the counter, where Greg was chatting with the barista, his posture far too casual. She lowered her voice. "You need to be careful with that one."

Charlotte frowned. "What are you talking about?"

"That's Greg," Bev said, her tone sharp now. "The guy who caused a scene at the Christmas market—remember? His dog tore through the stalls, ruined half the displays, and he didn't even apologize. When I tried to photograph his license plate, he got aggressive, lunging at me in the parking lot. And, Lottie, he's got a reputation. Not a good one."

Charlotte's stomach knotted. "Are you sure it's the same man?"

"I'd stake my life on it," Bev said, scrolling her phone and holding it up. "Here—these are the pictures I took that day. It's him, alright. He's trouble, Lottie. Trouble that may look good at first but leaves a mess behind."

Charlotte stared down at her coffee, disappointment clouding her face. Her instincts about men had failed her before—looks like she'd been wrong again.

As Greg walked toward their table with two refills in hand, Bev said a quick goodbye and scooted out the door. Charlotte lifted her cup, considering whether to mention the Christmas market disaster.

Greg leaned back in his chair, his confident smile firmly in place. "So," he said, "where were we?"

She forced a small smile, setting her cup back down. "I think you were telling me about your last trip to the coast?"

"Ah, right." His voice brightened as he launched into a story about his sailing adventures, but Charlotte's attention wavered. Bev's words echoed in her mind, mingling with her doubts. She nodded at the right moments, her fingers idly tracing the rim of her plastic lid, yet the conversation drifted past her like a radio playing softly in another room.

Greg didn't seem to notice her drifting focus, his excitement bubbling over as he talked. Charlotte caught herself watching him, her first impression of his effortless charm now clouded by Bev's revelation. She couldn't shake the feeling that, for all his charisma, she had missed seeing him for who he was.

Charlotte hesitated, debating whether to let it go or hear his side of the story. His response could be revealing, and she needed to know more.

"I remember hearing about what happened at the Christmas market," she said, keeping her tone light but curious. "It must've been...quite the scene."

He chuckled, shaking his head. "Poor Max couldn't help himself. The organizers left the doors wide open with all those food smells wafting out. What did they expect? Honestly, they should've been more careful. If you ask me, it's their fault for not thinking it through."

She nodded slowly, trying to process his response. The way he shifted the blame so easily left her unsettled. Greg's charm remained intact, his grin persuasive—but his explanation gave her pause.

"Right," she murmured, her gaze dropping to her coffee.

Greg leaned forward, his grin returning as he switched topics. "Anyway, let's not talk about that. I'd much rather hear more about you."

Charlotte nodded, forcing another smile, but her thoughts lingered elsewhere. For all his charm, Greg's easy deflection left her wondering just how wrong she'd been about him.

"I have little to tell," Charlotte said, glancing sideways. "I lived in England most of my life, and when my daughter moved here, I followed her. Now I help my friend Stewart on the farm."

Greg peppered her with questions—"Do you have a boyfriend? Ever marry? What do you like to do for fun?"

She replied with short answers, careful not to share much. In the café's hustle and bustle, it was easy to keep it that way.

He drained the last of his coffee, setting the cup down with a flourish. "This was nice. We should do it again—maybe dinner next time?"

Charlotte froze for a moment, the invitation hanging in the air like a challenge, even though she'd expected this. Bev's warning echoed in her mind, and Greg's own words didn't help.

"Oh," she said lightly, searching for the right excuse. "Coffee was manageable, but with Stewart needing extra help these days... let's just say there aren't enough hours in the day."

"Stewart?" Greg asked, raising an eyebrow.

Charlotte nodded, keeping her tone casual. "He's been juggling a lot, and I told him I'd step in where I could. He's been so supportive lately, you know? Hard to find that sort of... kindness."

Greg's smile tightened, but he shrugged. "Well, let me know. I'd hate to get in the way of your work."

"She smiled politely, feeling relieved as he gathered his things and stood. "Thanks for the coffee," she said.

WHEN HE WAS GONE, Charlotte let out a deep sigh. Her brief thoughts turned to Stewart—his empathy when she'd told him about Fred's passing, the way he looked out for her when Greg had been watching her too closely. Back then, it seemed like a simple act of kindness. But now, the way Greg shifted the blame so easily, Stewart's quiet concern felt different.

Maybe she wasn't as alone in this as she'd thought.

STROLLING across the freshly mowed lawn toward her home, Charlotte spotted Stewart gathering a bouquet of alstroemeria beneath the yellow plum tree. "Gorgeous day, isn't it, Stewart?"

she called out, feeling good about having stood her ground with Greg.

"This July's been just about perfect," Stewart replied, still crouching. "You look lovely this morning," he added, smiling warmly.

"Why, thank you," she said, a little surprised. She wasn't used to compliments from Stewart, who usually saw her in work clothes. But today, she'd dressed up for her date with Greg. Now, she couldn't wait to change.

"You know," Charlotte said, "I've been admiring those flowers since the first time I saw them in your kitchen. It's nice that you always have a fresh bouquet in the house."

Stewart smiled, looking up at her. "They were Amelia's favourite. Every year, she couldn't wait for them to bloom. Alstroemeria filled our house all season long."

"That colour is striking," Charlotte said. "Sort of coral, isn't it?"

"Yes," Stewart agreed, his smile deepening. "That's what I'd call it. Hard to find, though. You'll see shades of yellow, purple, red, white, and maybe orange in the shops, but this one's rare."

Standing up, Stewart offered the bouquet to Charlotte. "Here," he said softly, "these are for you."

"Oh, no, Stewart; I couldn't," she said, picturing them already in a vase on her dining table.

"I insist," he said, a pleased expression spreading across his face. "As you can see, there's lots where they came from."

"Thank you. I love them—and now I know what they're called." Grasping the bouquet, Charlotte continued walking toward her house. "Have a good afternoon, Stewart. See you tomorrow."

~

WIPING DOWN THE COUNTER, Charlotte moved the old, hinged wood box aside, its rough surface catching slightly on the edge. She'd been tidying up Stewart's kitchen for what felt like ages, and the box, sitting untouched in the corner, was taking up valuable counter space. More than once, she'd wondered if it even needed to be there.

Swinging open the lid, she found it filled with handwritten recipe cards, the ink faded in places, but still legible. She shuffled through them, reading the titles of a few recipes she had never heard of before—probably old family favorites. Amelia's neat handwriting, a looping script, conveyed a sense of care that felt so... personal.

As she paused over a recipe for peach cobbler, Stewart's footsteps grew closer, and he stopped behind her. The silence between them thickened before he let out a deep sigh.

"I've been meaning to deal with that, but... " He trailed off. "... it's hard."

Charlotte closed the lid of the box gently, turning to face him. She nodded, understanding all too well what he meant.

"I thought it was Amelia's handwriting," she whispered, glancing at the box before meeting his eyes. "It's hard to let go of something so personal. Handwriting, it's just... It's so tied to the person, isn't it?"

Stewart didn't respond right away, but his shoulders eased slightly, as though her words had unlocked something he'd been holding back.

Charlotte reached for the box again, cradling it in her hands for a moment.

"I know it's important to you," she said carefully, "but it's been years, Stewart. I can't help but wonder... do you still need it here? In the kitchen, where it's no longer... useful?"

He looked at the box, then back at her, his expression uncertain.

"I don't know," he admitted. "I guess I'm not ready to let go of anything that reminds me of her. It's the only thing I have left of her... in some ways, it feels like if I move it, or get rid of it, I'm saying she's gone. I don't know how to do that." His voice cracked slightly at the end.

Charlotte's heart softened as she stepped closer, her voice low but steady.

"It's okay to let go of things, Stewart. Keeping it around just because it's tied to a memory doesn't mean you have to forget. But maybe it's time to think about where you keep it... somewhere more private. Somewhere it's not... in the way of your life now."

Stewart's gaze dropped to the box, and for a long moment, he didn't speak. Then, slowly, he nodded. "Maybe you're right. I've never thought about it like that."

Charlotte gave him a small, understanding smile. "It's okay to hold on to the memories, Stewart. Just not the burden."

Stewart met her gaze, his expression grateful but still touched with sadness. "Thank you," he murmured, his words carrying more than just gratitude. Charlotte squeezed his arm lightly in return, knowing that this was more than just a conversation about a box of recipe cards. It was about moving forward without losing the past.

Glancing at the clock, Stewart said, "Would you mind answering the door for Jake Graham this morning? He's prepaid for choice cuts from a side of beef and said he'd stop by before noon."

"Of course," Charlotte said. "Where can I find it?"

"It's in the basement freezer, clearly marked with his name. Don't worry, he'll carry it upstairs himself."

"Have you always raised beef cattle, Stewart?" Charlotte asked.

"Yes, I have. Back in the day, Jennie Mitchell's father, John, and I shared a herd—kept it on my farm. John was a dear friend—he and Kathleen, of course."

"Ah," Charlotte said with a nod. "So, you've been a friend of the Mitchell family for generations."

Stewart's face lit up with pride. "There's no family like the Mitchells," he said, "and now you are part of that family, too."

"I agree. I sure lucked out with them."

"Meant to be, I'd say," Stewart replied, his eyes holding a look Charlotte couldn't quite read. "Now," he continued, "I need to get out to the fields and check in with the farmhands. See you later, Charlotte."

Charlotte was scrubbing the upstairs bathroom when she heard pounding on the screen door, followed by a deep voice calling, "Anybody home?" Startled, she grabbed a towel to dry her hands and hurried downstairs.

"Be right there!" she called, her voice carrying through the house.

As she opened the screen door, a man with broad shoulders greeted her, his weathered yet strikingly handsome face framed by unruly hair that curled beneath the brim of a well-worn baseball cap. His dark eyes sparkled with mischief, and he extended a firm handshake.

"Hello, you must be Jake Graham," Charlotte said, stepping aside to let him in.

"That's right," he replied with an amiable smile that revealed perfectly straight teeth. "Here to pick up that side of beef."

"This way," she said, leading him down to the basement. She was acutely aware of his presence behind her, his boots thudding softly on the wooden steps. At the freezer, she opened the lid and stepped back.

"There you go," she said, pointing to the neatly labeled packages.

Jake reached in and retrieved the frozen beef, loading the packages in his arms with some effort. Back upstairs, he paused by the door, smiling again, and looked at her just a second longer than seemed natural.

"Thank you, Mrs. Owen. So nice to meet you," he said.

Charlotte blinked, surprised by the comment. She let out a soft laugh. "Oh, no," she said, shaking her head, "I'm not Stewart's wife—just helping out around here."

Jake raised an eyebrow, his smile lingering. "Ah, I see. Well, you have yourself a nice day, ma'am."

As she closed the door behind him, Charlotte replayed the interaction in her mind, noting the warmth in his gaze and his effortless charm. Later that afternoon, when Stewart came in from the fields, she recounted the encounter, her tone light and teasing.

"He's quite the charmer, that Jake Graham," she said, grinning. "And handsome, too."

Stewart didn't respond right away. He went quiet, his expression unreadable, and busied himself with washing up at the sink. Charlotte thought she might have embarrassed him.

"But you know what he called me?" she added, leaning against the counter. "Mrs. Owen! Can you imagine?"

At that, Stewart's head lifted, and a slow smile formed on his lips. "Is that so?" he said with a hint of amusement.

As Charlotte finished tidying up the kitchen, Stewart returned, wiping his hands with a rag. "You know," he said, his voice casual, "you're welcome to eat dinner here with me, Monday to Thursday. Why make my dinner and then go home and make yours?"

Charlotte hesitated, but his reasoning was sound. "Well," she said with a small smile, "that makes sense."

He nodded, appreciating her understanding. "Glad you agree," he replied.

By the time Stewart came in from feeding the animals, she'd set a second place at the table. Over dinner, the conversation turned to her house, and she mentioned a flickering light in the hallway.

Stewart nodded thoughtfully. "Tell you what," he said, setting down his fork, "I'll come by after dinner and look at it for you."

"Really?" Charlotte asked, surprised.

"Sure," he said with a faint smile. "What are neighbors for?"

Charlotte felt the warmth in his tone and couldn't help but enjoy their easy rapport.

SATURDAY ARRIVED WITH CLEAR SKIES, perfect for the roadside stand. Charlotte stepped into a pair of denim shorts that showed off her shapely legs, her fitted top dipping just low enough to tease without being over-the-top. As she tied her hair back, she admired her reflection in the bathroom mirror, her smile radiating confidence. Over the past few months, she had grown comfortable in her skin—more alive, more herself than she had been in years. She wasn't looking for attention, exactly, but when it came, she found she enjoyed it.

At the stand, the buzz of chatter filled the air as locals and tourists browsed through baskets of fresh produce, baked goods, and jars of honey. Charlotte's smile was warm and inviting, her laughter light as she answered questions about the best ways to cook zucchini or preserve strawberries. Now and then, she caught a glance—some subtle, some not—from a male shopper. And she didn't mind.

"Excuse me, miss," one man said, stepping closer to her. His smile was friendly, his eyes appreciative. "I haven't seen you around here before. Are you new to the area?"

Charlotte flushed lightly but smiled with pleasure. Miss. It had been years since anyone had called her that. "Not exactly new," she said with a playful shrug. "But I guess you could say I've been... rediscovering the area."

Stewart, standing nearby with his arms crossed, watched the exchange. His jaw tightened. The man's tone was respectful enough, but there was something in the way he lingered, his gaze dropping ever so slightly before meeting Charlotte's eyes again. That made Stewart bristle.

When the man finally moved on, Charlotte glanced over at Stewart. "What's that look for?" she teased, tilting her head.

"Nothing," he grumbled, shifting his weight. "Just wondering if I should start charging admission for the stand."

Charlotte laughed, the sound soft and free. "Oh, come on, Stewart. It's harmless."

He didn't respond, but the tight set of his jaw remained.

Later that afternoon, as they packed up the stand, Charlotte stretched her arms overhead, her skin glowing from the sun. "You know," she said, "I've started swimming in the lake. You should come with me sometime."

Stewart hesitated, rubbing the back of his neck. "The lake's too cold for me," he said, the excuse sounding weak even to his ears.

Charlotte smirked. "Cold, huh? That's a shame. Guess I'll have to find someone braver to join me."

She caught a flash of something—jealousy, maybe—in his expression.

"Maybe," he muttered, then added quickly, "But how about fishing instead? Early tomorrow morning. We'll catch something good for dinner."

Her eyes lit up. "Fishing, huh? I'm game. You better show me how it's done, though."

∾

THE NEXT DAY, they returned to her kitchen with two freshly caught salmon. The mood was light as Charlotte pulled out cutting boards and knives. She insisted on trying her hand at filleting one fish, despite Stewart's protests.

"Careful with that knife," he warned, watching her grip the handle a little too loosely.

"I've got this," she said confidently—right before the blade slipped and nicked her finger.

"Charlotte!" Stewart was at her side in an instant, grabbing a clean towel to press against the cut. She wavered, her face going pale as she leaned against the counter.

"I think I might—" she whispered, but her knees buckled slightly.

"I've got you," he said firmly, steadying her with one arm while keeping pressure on her finger. "Lie down." He guided her to the sofa and raised her legs to increase the blood flow to her head, waiting until she recovered.

As she felt better, he helped her sit up slowly and poured her a glass of water. "Now," he said, smiling warmly. "You just relax here, and I'll finish the fish."

Charlotte smiled up at him, her breath evening out. "You're... good at this," she whispered.

"At what?" he asked, glancing up.

"Being steady. Calm. Like nothing rattles you."

He shrugged, a faint blush creeping up his neck. "You get used to it, running a farm."

But Charlotte shook her head. "No. It's more than that. You're... dependable. Reassuring." She paused, looking down at her bandaged finger, then back at him. "I've missed that. For a long time."

Stewart didn't reply immediately, but her words seemed to settle with him. "You deserve better, Lottie," he said, squeezing her shoulder.

Charlotte had grown tired after their fishing trip and her

near-fainting spell, so she rested on the sofa while Stewart prepared dinner. She closed her eyes and dozed off until a gentle tap on her arm woke her.

"It's ready, dear," he said, then caught his mistake. "Sorry," he said, "I didn't mean to call you *dear*."

"It's quite all right, Mr. Lovely," she replied, a warm smile spreading across her face. "I understand how you meant it—sincerely—not in that condescending way some people use to elevate themselves."

"What do you mean?" he asked, curious.

"Oh, it probably doesn't happen to you," Charlotte mused. Sometimes strangers call me 'dear.' How can someone feel endeared to me when they don't even know me? And when it's someone my age—or worse, much younger—it just feels patronizing."

Stewart chuckled. "I see. A woman's world, I guess."

They settled at the dining table to enjoy the meal Stewart had prepared. As they ate, he talked about Amelia. "She had the most beautiful herb garden, built up over the years. It was her pride and joy," he said, his voice softening. "Lavender, rosemary, thyme, tarragon—she had a way with it all. The herbs became more than part of her garden. They were her signature."

"She sounds remarkable," Charlotte said, leaning forward. Her mind flashed back to her first day pulling weeds in that very garden when she realized the depth of Stewart's loss. She remembered his pacing on the lawn, his hand on his jaw, the deep furrow in his brow. Now it all made sense. "Tell me more about her garden."

"Amelia used those herbs in nearly every meal," he continued. "Lamb casserole always had rosemary. Sage and onion stuffing for pork. Tarragon mustard sauce for grilled tenderloin. She had such a talent for pairing flavors."

Charlotte's stomach tightened slightly. Could her dinners

ever compare? "It all sounds delicious," she said, willing away her doubts. "Please go on."

"But it was her lavender that everyone remembered most," Stewart said with a wistful smile. "She dried it into sachets for her friends, to keep in closets or tuck under pillows for better sleep. And her lavender butter sauce for baked salmon—that was something else."

"She was a gourmet," Charlotte remarked, her admiration tinged with a trace of self-doubt. How could anyone compete with such a legacy? "You paint a picture of an idyllic time. Are you sure this person was real?" she joked.

Stewart glanced down, his expression caught somewhere between pride and embarrassment. Well, it was part of our lives for twenty-seven years."

"That's a long time," Charlotte said, deciding to take a chance. "But sometimes, even wonderful memories can hold us back."

Stewart sat quietly, considering her words. "Memories of Amelia do not exactly haunt me, but I think I've been holding on too tightly," he said finally. "Maybe it's time I moved on."

"Do you think talking about her helps?" she asked gently.

"Maybe," he admitted. "I've kept it all in like nothing could touch what we had. But I see now that's not the best way to handle grief."

"I admire your honesty," Charlotte replied, her voice gentle. "If there's anything I can do to help, just let me know."

"You're already helping," he said, meeting her eyes. "You being here makes a difference."

Her breath caught at the quiet sincerity in his voice. "How so?" she asked.

"It's hard to explain," he murmured, standing to clear the dishes. At the sink, he frowned at a dripping faucet.

"Oh, I meant to tell you about that," Charlotte said. "I hate wasting water, especially on the island."

Stewart twisted the tap off, then drew it slightly back toward himself. The dripping ceased. "Problem solved," he said with a grin. "For now, anyway. I'll take a proper look this weekend."

Charlotte smiled. Stewart might still carry the weight of the past, but in small, thoughtful ways, he moved forward—and that gave her hope.

~

THE NEXT EVENING, at dinner, Stewart shared more stories about Amelia. "She loved to paint in oil," he said, his voice warm with remembrance.

Charlotte fought to keep her expression neutral, hiding the fact that she had already glimpsed the paintings in the locked room. She leaned forward. "Do you have any of her work?"

Stewart's face softened. "I do," he said.

"I've been taking lessons from Bev—she sells her paintings at the summer market," Charlotte continued. "I'm not very good, but I love painting. I bet Amelia was talented."

"She was," Stewart said with a small smile, a hint of pride in his voice. "Would you like me to show you her work after dinner?"

Charlotte's breath caught. "I'd love that," she said, her voice brimming with joy. This felt like a breakthrough. Encouraged, she asked, "Does this mean I get to see inside the locked room?"

Stewart smiled. "There's a lot of history in there," he said. "You'll have the honor of being the only one to cross that threshold besides me in a very long time."

"I'm honored, Stewart," Charlotte said, her voice steady despite feeling emotional. "Truly. It means the world that you trust me enough to share what's sacred to you."

After finishing dinner and tidying the kitchen together, Stewart took her hand and led her down the hall to the locked door. As he turned the key, the old mechanism clicked with a sound that seemed to echo through the quiet house. When the door creaked open, brittle fragments of dried leaves scattered to the floor. The air inside was cooler than Charlotte remembered from her secret visit.

Stewart flicked on the overhead light. Charlotte folded her arms and shivered. "Brrrr," she said lightly.

Stewart chuckled and wrapped an arm around her shoulders. "We'll warm up in a minute," he said, guiding her toward the wall of paintings. They stood side by side, gazing at the vibrant colors and intricate details.

Charlotte gently pulled away and studied each painting, commenting on the composition, the colour choices, and Amelia's talent. "If only I could paint like this someday," she said.

She moved closer to the paintings, admiring the bold brushstrokes and thoughtful composition. "These are breathtaking," she said, her voice full of awe.

When she'd finished admiring the artwork, her eyes drifted to the dressing table. Stewart's posture stiffened, revealing his hesitation.

Charlotte approached the red sundress hanging nearby, brushing her thumb and forefinger gently against the fabric. "This is beautiful," she said softly. "An example of her style, I take it?"

"She loved dressing up," Stewart replied, his voice warm, filled with the comfort of fond memories. "Any special occasion had her dressed to the nines. There weren't many places to go on the island, but she lived for our trips to Vancouver and the big city—though only for a while. She was a country girl at heart."

"I get that," Charlotte said, smiling. "Who wouldn't love it here on Sunrise Island? I feel like I've died and gone to heaven." She froze, realizing too late the words she'd chosen.

But Stewart didn't flinch. Instead, he gave her a small,

understanding smile. "Would you like to see more of her dresses?"

"Only if you're comfortable," Charlotte said, sensing how deeply personal this was for him.

Stewart opened the closet door and gestured toward the neatly preserved garments. "I kept the ones tied to the happiest memories," he said. "Over time, some of those memories faded, and I held onto these as a safeguard. But now I see how foolish that was. Fabric fades, photos fade. But memories? The good ones, the meaningful ones—they're always here." He placed his hand on his heart. "Amelia will always be here."

Charlotte closed the closet door gently. "You're right, Stewart. For me, it's the opposite. I have terrible memories of my life with Fred that I work to let go of, even though they'll never fully disappear. But they don't hold me back anymore. The wonderful memories? I treasure them, but I'm okay with letting them fade, too. They belong to a different chapter of my life."

Charlotte looked up, meeting his eyes. They were tender, searching. Without overthinking, she raised her hands to his face, drawing him closer. Their lips met, tentatively at first, then with growing intensity. The embrace deepened, pulling them into a moment that felt timeless.

In the quiet of the house, surrounded by Amelia's lingering presence, they found a closeness unburdened by the past. For the first time, Charlotte felt that Amelia's memory wasn't a barrier—but a bridge.

THE NEXT DAY AT DINNER, Charlotte eagerly shared a story about her latest date, a one-time event.

"Over appetizers," she said with a laugh, "he made a phone call right there at the table—at The Oystercatcher, of all places. Then he brushed it off with, 'Business never sleeps.'"

Stewart laughed heartily, tilting his head back. "I bet that made you feel valued," he said sarcastically.

"Let's put it this way: I ordered extra champagne, secretly toasting the fact that this would be the last time I'd waste another minute on that jerk."

Charlotte had baked a peach pie to celebrate the upcoming weekend—at least that's what she told Stewart. Secretly, though, it was her way of marking his change of heart about memorabilia. She wanted to keep the momentum going, and after dessert, she delicately asked, "Stewart, I was wondering if you'd like me to donate Amelia's belongings?"

"I was hoping you'd ask, Charlotte. It's not something I could bring myself to do, despite my new perspective on holding on to things. But I can't be the one to do it."

"I understand. If it's okay with you, I'll take them tomorrow morning," she said, hoping he wouldn't change his mind.

To her delight and surprise, he replied, "How about we meet in that room tomorrow as soon as you get here? I want your opinion on how we can repurpose it. I know you'll have some good ideas."

At 8:00 a.m., Charlotte arrived to find the door to Amelia's room slightly ajar. She hesitated for a moment, sensing the significance of the task ahead. As she stepped inside, she saw Stewart standing near Amelia's dresser, his fingers brushing its surface. Beside him, the silver hairbrush with strands of Amelia's hair sat on the polished wood. His shoulders were stiff, his expression distant.

"Good morning," Charlotte said softly, not wanting to startle him.

He turned to her with a faint smile. "Morning. I thought I'd get a head start, but it's harder than I expected."

Charlotte approached gently, placing a reassuring hand on his arm. "It's never easy to let go, Stewart. But you're taking a brave step today." She glanced at the dresser. "Is there anything in there you'd like to keep?"

He nodded and opened one drawer, carefully removing a small velvet box and a stack of photographs. "Some of her jewelry and these pictures. The rest... I think it's time." He placed the keepsakes in the chest by the window, where he kept other cherished items of Amelia's.

While he worked through the contents of the other drawers, Charlotte crossed to the closet. The dresses hung neatly, still carrying a faint trace of perfume. Charlotte's heart ached for Stewart as she carefully removed them, folding each one with reverence. She placed them in a large box she'd brought for donation.

"Charlotte," Stewart said after a moment, his voice steadier now. "What do you think about donating the dresser, too? Once it's empty, of course."

She smiled, encouraged by his suggestion. "I think that's a wonderful idea. It'll make a fresh start for this room."

Together, they cleared out the remaining items, with Stewart lingering over an unfinished painting that Amelia had been working on. He traced the brushstrokes with a bittersweet expression before setting it aside to keep.

By mid-morning, they had emptied the dresser and loaded it into Stewart's pickup truck, along with the box of dresses, ready to be taken to the Salvation Army. Charlotte stood by the window, gazing at the heavy drapes that darkened the space. "If it's all right with you, I'd like to give the room a thorough cleaning. I'll even tackle these windows."

Stewart paused, then nodded slowly. "That sounds good. Let's start with this." He stepped forward, his hands lingering on the thick fabric before drawing the drapes back. Sunlight streamed into the room as he raised the blinds, illuminating the space with soft morning light.

Charlotte felt a quiet triumph as she watched him take that step.

"The room feels lighter, even though it's still filled with memories, don't you think, Stewart?" she asked, her voice warm with encouragement.

He turned to her, a hint of gratitude in his eyes. "You're right. It feels better. Thank you, Charlotte, for everything."

"I'm happy to help," she said, her eyes filled with tenderness. Guiding him through such a delicate process felt like an important step forward for them both.

As Stewart left to deliver the donations, Charlotte lingered in the room, taking in the changes. Sunlight streamed through the windows, casting a gentle glow over the walls. For the first time, she could imagine this space becoming something entirely new—a reflection of the changes unfolding in their lives.

AFTER STEWART DELIVERED THE DONATIONS, he stopped by the Mitchell farm. Jennie was in the vegetable garden, her Dutch hoe slicing through the soil. He parked his truck in the circular driveway, the gravel crunching under his tires, and walked over to join her.

"Mornin', Jennie," he said with a broad smile. "I figured I'd find you here—working your magic in the garden, as usual." He raised his brows teasingly.

"From one farmer to another," she said with a grin, "the work never stops. But we wouldn't have it any other way, would we?"

"Oh, I don't know about that, Jen," he said with a light

chuckle, his tone shifting. "The older I get, the more I wonder about that."

Jennie didn't miss the change in his voice. She studied him for a moment before asking, "How's it going with Lottie? Is she a big help?"

Stewart's face softened, his eyes warming. "Oh, I've found a new lease on life with her around," he said, his words slow and reflective.

They talked briefly about the benefits of having hired help and how much he enjoyed Charlotte's company. But as the conversation shifted, Stewart's usual ease seemed to fade. He grew quieter, his posture less confident.

Jennie paused, setting down her hoe. She eyed him closely, sensing something was off. "What's on your mind, Stewart?"

He shifted his weight from one foot to the other, crossing his arms over his chest. "Nothing wrong, Jen. Just... puzzling, I guess." He took a deep breath, his voice quieter now. "I think I'm developing feelings for Lottie."

Jennie raised an eyebrow. "Is that so?"

Stewart exhaled softly. "After Amelia died, I thought that chapter of my life was closed. Then Lottie came along, and—well, I found myself jealous when other men looked at her. And I hardly even knew her! It caught me off guard."

Jennie's voice was gentle as she nodded. "She's a stunning woman," she said, her eyes alight with warmth.

A trace of vulnerability crossed Stewart's face as he smiled. "She is. And it surprised me how much it got to me. We weren't even dating ..."

Jennie set her hoe aside, adjusting her cap as she listened intently. "Look, Stewart. We can't control how we feel. Feelings just... happen. There's no right or wrong about it."

Stewart exhaled, running a hand through his hair. "Yeah, I guess you're right. But it's been hard for me to move on, you know. I've spent so long with these walls up, thinking I was protecting myself. But Lottie somehow broke through them. And now I'm seeing that I was holding myself back from living, from...."

Jennie's expression softened, her eyes warm with understanding. "Well, it sounds like you've made some amazing progress, Stewart. I'm happy for you."

Stewart looked at her, a genuine smile spreading across his face. "Feels good," he said, his voice light. Then, with a slight pause, he added, "I donated her things to charity before I came here. It felt right."

Jennie nodded, her smile tender. "How fitting. Amelia was always so generous, and it's nice to think her kindness is still making a difference."

Stewart's expression softened, as though he'd found a sense of resolution about the past.

Jennie studied him for a moment before speaking again, her voice warm and genuine. "You know, Stewart, now that you're letting go of the past, I think you might just find yourself open to new possibilities—new love, new happiness."

Stewart gave a short, thoughtful laugh and leaned in to embrace her. "I'll keep that in mind, Jen. Say hi to Kathleen for me, will you?"

As Stewart climbed into his truck and pulled away, he saw Jennie standing at the edge of the garden, a grin on her face. He couldn't help but think that, for the first time in a long while, he was finally making progress. Jennie had been where he was now—thinking she'd never love again after Derrick's sudden death. And yet, here she was, smiling, with Clay by her side. Maybe it wasn't too late for him, either."

THE LATE AFTERNOON sun blazed through the dirty windows of what had once been a room shrouded in secrecy. The faint mustiness of long-closed spaces still lingered in the air. Charlotte glanced around, taking in the faded floral wallpaper and the worn carpet, relics of a life frozen in time.

Footsteps drew her attention to the doorway, and Stewart stepped in, a smile spreading across his face. "Let there be light," he said.

It's bigger than I expected," she murmured, her gaze lingering on the space that now felt full of possibility. "It could be anything we want it to be now."

"Well," Stewart said, clearing his throat as he stepped closer, "it could. Guest room, office... heck, even a fancy bathroom." He glanced at Charlotte, his heart pounding. "Or, uh, something we'd both use. Like a gym?"

Charlotte raised an eyebrow. "A gym?"

"Emily mentioned it," Stewart explained quickly, words tumbling out. "You know, strengthening my muscles and all that. She said it'd help with my joints. And I thought..." He trailed off, scratching the back of his neck.

"You figured I might join you?" Charlotte asked, arms crossed.

"Yeah," Stewart said, his voice softening. "I just thought it could be something we do together."

"I like it," Charlotte interrupted, a smile forming. "I think it's a great idea."

Relief washed over Stewart, and he chuckled nervously. "Good. That's... good."

Charlotte bit her lower lip, her eyes narrowing. "I notice we're both using the 'we' word a lot lately. Don't you?"

"I know," Stewart said, a little sheepishly. "It just comes out naturally. Can't argue with feelings, right?"

Charlotte stepped closer, resting her hand on his shoulder. "I'm not arguing," she said, her voice soft. "You sure about this? About us?"

Stewart met her gaze, his heart thumping. "I'm sure," he

said firmly. "But I get it if you're not. I mean, I'm an old farmer set in my ways. You're... well, you."

She laughed softly, shaking her head. "Me? I'm just a woman trying to figure out how to trust again. Fred wasn't great at letting me take the lead."

"Then you should," Stewart said quickly, his tone earnest. "Take the lead, I mean. This room. Us. Whatever you want."

Charlotte studied him, caught between hesitation and hope. "What do you hope for in a relationship with me, Stewart?"

His answer came without hesitation. "Companionship—someone to share life's joys and sorrows, share meals, and share a bed... if that's what you want."

"I want all of that, Stewart." Charlotte's voice softened as she added, "I don't do well living alone. And, if I have the choice, I'll take a salt-of-the-earth guy like you any day over those yahoos I've been dating. I'm too old for games, and after my first marriage, you and this island? You're a dream come true."

Stewart's grin spread slowly, warm and genuine. "We can have a platonic relationship if that's what you want," he said tenderly, his voice low. "It's entirely your choice, sweetheart. But, so you know... I'm still more than capable in every sense."

Charlotte smirked, a spark of resolve in her voice as she said, "Alright. Let's do this. A repurposed room and a repurposed couple." She took a deep breath. "You and I, the Lord and Lady of Owen Manor."

Stewart's grin deepened, although a hint of playfulness danced in his eyes. "You sure?"

Without responding, Charlotte cupped his face in her hands and pulled him in for a kiss. At first, it was gentle, a testing of the waters. Then, the kiss deepened, passion sweeping them both away. When they finally pulled apart,

Charlotte let out a breathless laugh. "Wow. I haven't felt like this since I was in college."

Stewart's eyes twinkled. "I'm not looking back, dear. I'm living right here, right now. And that kiss we just shared? I want more of that. Just like that."

Together, they tossed around ideas for the room—fresh paint instead of wallpaper, bare windows to let the light stream in, and simple touches that felt like them. Over the next few weeks, they stripped the walls, pulled up the worn carpet, and refinished the floors. The air, once still and quiet, now echoed with their laughter and easy banter, filling the space with warmth. But the transformation wasn't just physical. With every brushstroke, every shared glance, the room—and their bond—grew into something new, vibrant, and full of promise.

When the work was finally done, they stood side by side in the middle of the room, taking it all in. The walls gleamed with a soft, inviting hue, and sunlight poured through the uncovered windows, bathing the space in warmth. On one wall, Amelia's paintings hung in careful arrangement—a nod to the past, adding beauty without overshadowing the room's fresh start.

Stewart turned to her, his expression thoughtful. "You know," he said quietly, "I don't think I could've done this without you."

Charlotte smiled, her eyes warm. "Of course, you could have. But I'm glad you didn't have to."

He reached for her hand, giving it a gentle squeeze. "Thank you," he said, his eyes steady.

"For what?"

"For showing me that there's still more to build. And for being brave enough to do it with me."

Charlotte leaned in, kissing him lightly. When she pulled back, her voice was steady but full of emotion. "We're in this together, Stewart. That's what makes it worth it."

~

AS THE MONTHS PASSED, Charlotte and Stewart grew inseparable. Together, they planted a row of poplar trees. "With time and care, they'll outlast both of us," Stewart said.

They discovered a shared love for cooking, often choosing Charlotte's well-designed kitchen for their culinary adventures.

"I have little to clean in your kitchen anymore, Stewart," she said one morning as she tidied up. "We spend more time in my kitchen than in yours."

Stewart chuckled. "We spend more time in your entire house, I'd say."

"Yeah," she teased, a playful glint in her eye. "We might as well move in together."

Stewart paused, her words hanging in the air. "You mean... try living together?"

"That's one way to put it," she replied, her tone light, although an edge of uncertainty crept in.

The room fell silent. Stewart sat back, a quiet grin spreading across his face. Charlotte suddenly felt as though she'd said too much—but then Stewart leaned forward, his voice steady and warm.

"You know, honey, I've been thinking about just that. Would you be willing to try?"

Charlotte blinked, surprised. Her thoughts swirled: *He chose me when he opened that closed room and opened his heart to me... But am I ready to commit to a man twenty-nine years older?*

When she didn't answer right away, Stewart filled the gap. "Jennie tells me Patrick's looking for a place. With Kyla expecting another baby, they'll outgrow that little cottage soon. And with Clay living at the farm, I think Patrick feels like he never really left home."

Charlotte tilted her head, a teasing smile playing on her

lips. "So, for purely practical reasons, you want to rent out your house to Patrick and move in with me? All for convenience?"

"Exactly," Stewart replied, his grin stretching wider. "It has nothing to do with the fact that I'm completely head over heels for you or that I want to spend the rest of my life with you."

Charlotte's expression softened as she reached for his hand. "All I want for Christmas—and forever—is you by my side."

STEWART OPENED the lid of a velvet box, revealing a thick gold chain resting against the white silk lining. The pendant—a blue topaz oval framed by a delicate ring of diamonds—was elegant, but it was the gold chain that truly caught the light, shimmering with a warm brilliance.

"Full disclosure—this was Amelia's," he said calmly. Thankfully, he seemed unaware that Charlotte had already glimpsed the piece when she snuck into the secret room.

Charlotte drew in a sharp breath, her eyes locked on the necklace. "It looks like it's fit for a queen," she whispered.

He smiled, eyes tender, and reached for her hand. "You are my queen."

6

BEV

Bev had made it her habit to enjoy lunch at the Treehouse Café every Wednesday. Today, she chose a spot outdoors under an umbrella as the sun blazed overhead. Without family commitments or pressing obligations, she was free to linger—and listen to the gossip.

"You know, they've moved in together—can you believe it?" said a woman in blue sweats, her cup halfway to her lips.

The woman in green nearly choked on her coffee. "You're kidding, right? He looks old enough to be her father."

She didn't need names to know they were talking about Stewart and Charlotte.

"It's such a shame," Blue Sweats said, lowering her voice conspiratorially. "He and Amelia were perfect together. I'm sure she's turning over in her grave."

"Yes," Green Sweats added, her tone sharp. "Amelia was a proper lady. She didn't deserve this."

Bev's jaw tightened. Of course—it was them. *The self-appointed town gossip duo.* She glanced at the server delivering their bill, waiting for her moment. As soon as the women tucked their credit cards away, Bev rose and strolled over to their table.

"Excuse me, ladies," she said, offering a faint smile.

Blue sweats lit up. "Bev, how lovely to see you! It's been ages, hasn't it?" Her lower lip curled back to reveal a row of perfect teeth.

Not long enough, Bev thought, but didn't say. Instead, she slid onto the bench beside Green Sweats. "I couldn't help overhearing your conversation about Stewart and Lottie."

"Lottie—is that her name?" Green Sweats wrinkled her nose as if she'd caught a bad smell.

"Yes," Bev said, ignoring the jab. "She's kind, hardworking, and has been a great help to Stewart—who, as you pointed out, is getting on in years."

"Well, he is," Blue Sweats said, her tone dripping with mock concern. "What is he now... seventy-five? And she's, what, in her forties?"

"Maybe," Bev replied. "Not that it matters. I haven't seen Stewart this happy in years."

Green Sweats gave a derisive snort. "I bet."

Bev leaned forward, her tone steady but firm. "Their relationship is no one's business but theirs. If they've found love—especially later in life—why not celebrate that instead of tearing it down?"

Blue Sweats pursed her lips. "It's just... the age gap. Don't you think it's extraordinary?"

Bev exhaled sharply, her patience thinning. "Extraordinary? Sure. But so is love. And Stewart and Lottie are two of the kindest, most genuine people I know. They don't deserve this kind of judgment."

She stood, brushing invisible crumbs from her lap.

"And if you're looking for something more productive to do," she added, her voice cooling, "maybe organize a fundraiser for the couple whose house burned down. Or volunteer at the old folks' home on Waverly Street—you might meet some lonely people who don't have anyone to grow old with."

Without waiting for a response, Bev turned and walked away, veering sharply to the left to put as much distance as possible between herself and their whispers.

7

JENNIE

One Year Later

Jennie adjusted Alexa's veil, her fingers lingering on the intricate lace. Catching Alexa's reflection in the mirror, she smiled, her hazel eyes shining with the joy of the moment.

"You look breathtaking," Jennie murmured, her voice thick with emotion.

Alexa turned, her hands brushing Jennie's. "Mom, what's the secret to a happy marriage?"

Jennie's smile deepened as she paused to consider the question, touched that Alexa would seek her wisdom. Memories of her life with Derrick surfaced—moments of laughter, heated arguments, and the quiet, steady rhythms that shaped their years together. Bittersweet as they were, those memories now sat alongside the joy of the love she shared with Clay.

"Patience," Jennie said softly. "And trust. Never stop communicating, even when it's hard. And always make time for each other. That's what keeps love strong."

Alexa's expression brightened, her confidence blooming. "Thank you, Mom. Last night, when I saw you and Clay walking hand in hand toward the clifftop at sunset—like you've done so many times—I knew that's the kind of marriage I want for Kevin and me."

Jennie's eyes softened. "And I wish the same for you and Kevin. Mutual respect and open communication will carry you through anything life throws your way."

THE LATE SUMMER sun blazed high as Jennie stood on the shaded verandah, watching Kyla load Izzy and baby Luke into the golf cart. Two-year-old Izzy giggled, clutching a small basket of plums, while five-month-old Luke cooed happily in his seat.

"Got your helpers today?" Jennie teased, stepping closer with a smile.

Kyla grinned, brushing a strand of hair from her face. "The best sales team around. Who could resist buying produce from these two?"

Jude approached, wiping his hands on his jeans. "Morning, Jennie. When you have a moment, I'd like to share my plans for the organic vegetable garden."

"I'd love to hear them, Jude," Jennie said warmly. Her gaze shifted as he loaded a crate of heirloom tomatoes onto the cart. "How's it going with Stewart? Are you learning the ropes of raising beef cattle? Did you know my father and Stewart used to share a herd years ago?"

Jude chuckled. "Stewart's been great. I never imagined I'd know this much about cattle, but he's taught me plenty—and yes, he's shared quite a few stories about your father."

Jennie glanced toward the fields, where Clay stood surveying the dry grass. He caught her eye and gave a small wave before turning his attention back to the land.

"He's worried about the fire risk," Kyla said softly. "Water's so scarce this year, but he's planning to use the sprinklers sparingly—just enough to lower the danger."

Jennie nodded, a quiet admiration for Clay settling in her chest. His steady presence and thoughtful leadership had seen the farm through so many challenges. Now, it looked like the next generation was stepping into their roles, ready to carry on the legacy.

LATER THAT AFTERNOON, Jennie stopped by the Treehouse Café, hoping for a quiet cup of tea. Instead, she spotted Bev and Lottie at a corner table, deep in conversation about their next painting destination.

"Jennie!" Bev called, waving her over. "We're heading to Burgoyne Bay Park. Care to join us?"

Jennie hesitated, glancing at the sketchbook tucked in her bag. She'd been meaning to get back to painting but hadn't found the time.

"Come on," Lottie urged with an encouraging smile. "It'll do you good."

Jennie chuckled softly. "All right. Let me grab my things."

By mid-afternoon, the three women were at the park, their easels set up beneath towering trees. The bay's calm waters shimmered in the golden light, and Jennie's brush moved with a freedom she hadn't felt in years. Bev's laughter and Lottie's cheerful chatter filled the air, making the time feel both creative and restorative.

"Hey, why don't you join us next week, Jennie?" Bev asked, her blue eyes sparkling as the sunlight lit her vibrant red hair.

Jennie smiled, lowering her brush. "If I can't make it next week, I promise I'll join you before the end of the month. How's that?"

"Can't wait!" Lottie chimed in. "And you get to pick the location, okay?"

"As long as it's on Sunrise Island," Jennie said with a grin, "it'll be perfect."

~

THAT EVENING, Jennie carried a tray of tea to the verandah, where Kathleen sat in her favorite chair, a wool blanket tucked around her legs.

"Here you go, Mom," Jennie said, setting the tray on the small table.

Kathleen's hands cradled the warm cup as she sighed contentedly, her gaze sweeping over the farm. "Thank you, dear. Your father would be so proud of all of you. This place—his dream—it's thriving, just like he always hoped."

Jennie settled into the chair beside her, her eyes misting. "It hasn't always been easy, but we've had each other. That's what's made the difference."

Kathleen nodded, her smile soft and serene. "And it always will. This family... it's strong. Just look at Alexa and Kevin, Kyla and Jude. Even Patrick is finding his way. The future is bright."

Jennie's heart swelled with pride as she thought of the generations to come. Izzy and Luke would grow up surrounded by love and the land that had shaped their family. Emily and Nick's chiropractic clinic was thriving, drawing patients from neighboring islands, and their upcoming trip to Italy was a testament to their hard work and devotion.

As the sun dipped below the horizon, Jennie stood and draped an arm around Kathleen's shoulders. Together, they watched the golden light fade, the farm bathed in a gentle, amber glow.

Jennie let her thoughts drift over her life—the hard-won

victories, the trials that had shaped her, and the love that had been a constant through it all.

As the first stars emerged in the darkening sky, she felt a quiet certainty: the love that had carried them through the years would guide the generations yet to come.

I hope the Sunrise Island Series has brought laughter, inspiration, and perhaps a fresh perspective on the human experience.

Thank you for joining me on this journey.

Maren Hill

ACKNOWLEDGMENTS

A special thank you to Kelley York, Terri Morgans, Jane Litherland, and Stephanie Ferguson. Your unwavering support and encouragement continue to inspire me, and I am so grateful to have you on this journey with me.

ABOUT THE AUTHOR

<u>Maren Hill</u>

Captivated by the intrigue of everyday life, Maren Hill writes heartfelt, emotional stories that celebrate women and the relationships that shape their lives.

Quirky, good-hearted characters you'd love to know, and stories laced with romance, humor, compassion, and inspiration are trademarks of Maren Hill's books.

<u>J.D. Monk</u>

Written by children's book author JD Monk, *Slimy Slick* appeals to children and adults alike with fascinating facts about banana slugs.

"If you enjoy my books, please leave a review. There's nothing more motivational than positive reviews. Thank you!"

SUNRISE ISLAND SERIES PREQUEL

CLIFFHOUSE FOOTPRINTS
Book Description

Kathleen Mitchell longs to be a mother before her biological clock ticks out. After trying for two years, she and John consider adoption. She visualizes a newborn baby nestled in her arms, with skin as soft as the petals of a delicate flower. But when life takes an unexpected turn and Kathleen's eight-year-old nephew comes to live with them during his mother's battle with cancer, their plans are upended.

Amidst the emotional whirlwind of caregiving, Kathleen discovers profound truths about the essence of parental love—a love that transcends blood ties. From heartbreak to unexpected joys, their journey illuminates the transformative power of love and the resilience of the human spirit.

Cliffhouse Footprints, the Sunrise Island Series prequel, celebrates the undeniable force that drives parents to protect, nurture, and support their children through any circumstances.

Follow Kathleen in her transformative journey in this clean

women's fiction prequel, a celebration of those who care for children everywhere.

Scan the QR code to follow or see www.marenhill.com for details.

Be the first to know about new releases, cover reveals, discounts, giveaways, and outtakes from the author's life.

ALSO BY MAREN HILL

Cliffhouse Footprints

Cliffhouse by the Sea

Sunrise Island Sisters

Sunrise Island Christmas

Sunrise Island Celebrations

Nicole
The Troublemakers
Our Forever Place

Make a Spectacular Seashell Lamp
Sealed with a Kiss

SLIMY SLICK—NOT JUST FOR KIDS

The Nighttime Adventures of a Banana Slug

This captivating picture book appeals to kids and adults through multiple reads and is jam-packed with suspense, slime, and fun facts.

Join Slimy Slick on his exciting nighttime adventure through the countryside as he glides toward the tasty treat of his dreams. He encounters an earthworm and a shrew, but the real danger lies ahead. Will Slick's journey come to an abrupt end at the hands of a well-meaning boy whose mission is to capture and eliminate? Does he not understand Slick's important role in the ecosystem?

Readers learn about the clever design of the banana slug and how Slick uses his natural gifts to protect himself and navigate life in the wild.

Discover the world of Slimy Slick through a rainforest adventure that educates and entertains, emphasizing the importance of these fascinating creatures to our planet.

Perfect for:

• Parents and grandparents, science teachers, librarians, and educators

• Gifts for kids who love nature, rainforest animals, and learning more about the natural world and zoology

• Read-aloud family sharing

• Gaining environmental wisdom

• Understanding empathy and collaboration

www.ingramcontent.com/pod-product-compliance
Lightning Source LLC
Chambersburg PA
CBHW020658120726
47906CB00001B/326